THE NOCTURNALS

Book One

The Mysterious Abductions

Tracey Hecht

Fabled Films Press
New York

Published by Fabled Films LLC, New York

ISBN: 978-1-944020-02-6
Library of Congress Control Number: 2015957068

First Paperback Edition: April 2017

1 3 5 7 9 10 8 6 4 2
Cover Designed by Jaime Mendola-Hobbie
Jacket Art by Kate Liebman
Interior Book Design by Notion Studio
Typeset in Stemple Garamond, Mrs. Ant and Pacific Northwest
Printed by Everbest in China

FABLED FILMS PRESS
NEW YORK CITY

www.fabledfilms.com

For information on bulk purchases for promotional use please
contact Consortium Book Sales & Distribution Sales department
at Sales.Orders@cbsd.com or 1-800-283-3572

For Leo, of course.
But not without Sarah and Tommy.

Book One

The Mysterious Abductions

PROLOGUE

As the first light of day surged above the horizon, Tobin crept toward home. It had been a long night of foraging for food, and the pangolin was feeling tired. "Mmm." The anteater-like creature yawned and slumped at the base of a tree. "Perhaps I'll just take a quick rest...." Tobin's sleepy eyes drooped shut.

Suddenly, something heavy dropped right on his scaly head.

"Ouch!"

The confused pangolin reached for the greenish-yellow object and examined it with his taloned paws. "A pomelo!" he exclaimed. Eagerly, Tobin peeled back the fruit's thick, spongy rind and took a whiff with his keen, elongated snout. "Heavenly!" He sighed. "Absolutely heavenly!"

But before he could taste the fruit's citrusy flesh, a voice screeched down from above. "Thief!" it cried. "Strange creature with back of blades! How dare you steal the bounty of my tree?"

Tobin dropped the pomelo at once. He was so startled that a small, smelly poof escaped from his rear. "Oh dear," he mumbled.

"Pee-yew!" yelled the high-pitched voice.

Tobin looked up. A small, furry animal was perched in the branches, pinching his nose with one paw. He looked somewhat like a squirrel, with dark round eyes and a long furry tail.

"That stench! That odor! That tang!" The creature scrunched its face in disgust. "This calls for the flaps." With that, he extended his arms and legs, revealing the winglike skin that connected his limbs. Frantically, he fanned the still-stinky air.

"Oh my," remarked Tobin, staring at the unique appendages. "How elegant."

"Ah yes." The animal sighed. "We sugar gliders are impressive indeed." He puffed out his chest with pride. "Fine physique...fabulous facial features...phenomenal fitness!" Fueled by his own self-esteem, the sugar glider launched from his perch, allowing the wind to gather gracefully under his wings and carry him to the ground.

Tobin smiled and stepped toward his new acquaintance. He was just about to introduce himself properly when he heard another strange voice from the brush.

"Is there a problem?" it said.

The pangolin turned toward the sound. But this time he did not jump. In contrast to the sugar glider's shrill pitch, the voice he'd just heard was gentle and soft. Tobin stared into the foliage. "Who's there?" he asked.

Out of the green leaves emerged a slender red fox.

"Oh *mon dieu*!" The sugar glider swooned, clasping his hands to his heart. "Never have my big brown eyes beheld such beauty outside of my own reflection!" He approached the fox and dropped to one knee. "Allow me to introduce myself. I am Bismark: macho marsupial, sweetest of sugar gliders, and your one true love." Quickly, he snatched the pomelo from under the pangolin's nose and presented it to the fox. "For you, my lady."

The newcomer raised an eyebrow. This bold creature, despite standing on tiptoe, barely reached her knee. She turned to Tobin. "Is everyone all right here?" she asked, twitching her nose. "I thought I smelled trouble."

"*Si*, the stinky one woke me up just as I was about to fall asleep."

"Oh, um…excuse me," responded the pangolin, bashfully shrugging his scales. "I spray my defensive odor when I get scared." He blushed. "I'm sorry…I can't help it."

The fox looked down at Tobin with her almond-shaped eyes and gave a reassuring nod of her head.

The pangolin smiled. "I'm Tobin," he said, extending a paw.

"I am Dawn," said the fox.

The sugar glider wedged himself between his two new acquaintances. "But of course you are!" he exclaimed. "Dawn—the magnificent moment each day when I settle in for my daily renewal, my dream-filled slumbers, my sunlit sleep." Bismark bowed deeply. "Your glow rivals that of the full moon, my lady."

"You mean, you also sleep during the day?"

asked Tobin, turning to the sugar glider.

Bismark stood tall. "*Mais oui!*" he confirmed. "I am a night prowler. I find my beetles and bananas when the moon is bright and the mood is right." The sugar glider spun close to the fox. "And you, *mon amour?*"

"I maintain evening hours, as well," replied Dawn.

Tobin's eyes brightened. "We're all nocturnals! Awake at night, asleep by day."

Bismark beamed. "By the stars!" he declared, thrusting his fist toward the glimmering sky above. "We are animals *de la noche*, keepers of the night, a Nocturnal Brigade! We can be bold in adventure…we can be brave in challenge…we can be—"

"You can be dinner."

A sharp hiss pierced the quiet air. Quickly, the pangolin, sugar glider, and fox spun around. Behind them was a menacing black snake with a bright blue belly. Its dark tongue flicked in and out.

"Hate to break up this beautiful moment, but I'm getting hungry over here." It hissed, and without another word of warning, it sprang toward them, fangs bared.

At once, Tobin, Bismark, and Dawn cleared the hungry snake's path. With his flaps spread out wide, the sugar glider leapt back up into the tree. Tobin curled into a ball, shielding himself with his scales. And Dawn jumped to the side just in the nick of time; the serpent's breath was hot on her tail.

Fuming and famished, the snake reared its head, its yellow eyes blazing like flames. Then, something happened. As the snake sprang forth again, time seemed to slow. Bismark looked at Dawn. The fox drew toward Tobin. The pangolin curled even tighter. Somehow, they knew what to do.

As Tobin held his breath, Dawn cocked her leg and punted the pangolin. Whoosh! He flew through the air—a spinning ball of armor—forcing the snake to jump back. As the serpent reeled in shock, Bismark flew from his branch, his tiny fist clenched and ready.

"Hiiiiya!" With a high-pitched yelp, he knocked the snake square in the jaw.

The serpent hissed with rage and opened its mouth. But the fox had charged from behind, and before the snake could clamp down its jaws, Dawn clamped down hers…right on the snake's narrow tail. Round and round went the snake as the fox rotated her neck. And then, with a flick of her head, Dawn whipped the serpent back and flung it into the bushes.

Breathless and stunned, the fox, the pangolin,

and the sugar glider stared into the brush, ensuring the snake was scared off. Then, they turned to each other.

"Is everyone all right?" asked Dawn.

"Oh goodness!" gasped Tobin. "That all happened so fast. I didn't even have time to think."

Bismark's chest swelled with pride. "Who needs to think when we have instinct? We are the Nocturnal Brigade—we fit together like the moon and the stars, like the wind and the wing, like—"

"Like a team!" suggested Tobin.

"Like friends," said Dawn.

For a moment, the animals stood in meaningful silence: Bismark, tiny in height, but grand in gesture; Tobin, armored with scales, yet tender at heart; and Dawn, delicate in manner, but strong in wisdom.

Tobin grabbed the pomelo and broke it into three equal sections. Together, the threesome savored the sweet, fragrant fruit and watched the moon fade away. The night was drawing to a close, but their friendship—and their adventures—were just about to begin.

Chapter One
A SHRIEK IN THE NIGHT

"They're late!" exclaimed Bismark. The sugar glider paced the dark land, searching for his absent friends. "We agreed to meet promptly at dusk," he muttered to himself.

At last, a voice emerged from the brush. "Oh goodness!" it panted. Rubbing his eyes, the pangolin hurried into the clearing. "I'm so sorry. I overslept."

Bismark gave a slight roll of his oversized eyes. "I shall let it slide this time, though tardiness is quite unacceptable. The marsupial family is always prompt, always ready, always...*bonjour!*" His voice dropped in pitch as he caught sight of Dawn's red muzzle poking through the brush. "How are you, my tardy but captivating canine?"

The fox furrowed her brow. "Bismark," she said, "what are you wearing?"

The sugar glider spun, showcasing a shimmering blue snakeskin he wore on his back like a cape.

Tobin's eyes widened in admiration. "So shiny!" he said.

"Let's focus on my cape," replied Bismark. "But yes, my fur glimmers like polished amber!" Shooting a wink at the fox, the sugar glider licked his palms and smoothed his silver-gray coat.

"Bismark," said Dawn, "the costume. Why are you wearing that thing?"

The sugar glider gasped. "Retract that remark at once! This is no mere costume, no ordinary 'thing'." He shook his head in distaste. "What you see before you," he declared, "is the majestic uniform of our brilliant Brigade. Together we will confront the dangers that lurk in the shadows. With these around our shoulders, sparkling like the starry sky, we will bring hope and protection to all the animals of the night. And see?"

Bismark reached into the folds of his wingflap. "*Voila*! Two more for my favorite *amigos*."

Dawn and Tobin accepted the skins of deep blue and draped them around their necks.

"Stunning. Absolutely stunning!" crooned Bismark, circling the fox in her new garb. "Only the best of the best for my canine princess." Standing on tiptoe, the sugar glider placed his face just inches from Dawn's. "You know," he said, twirling his whiskers, "that blue-bellied black snake needed a little persuading to part with his precious skin." Bismark flexed his muscles and winked.

Dawn raised an eyebrow, unamused by the sugar glider's tall tale. Tobin, however, took the bait. "You went back and wrestled the blue-bellied black snake by yourself?" he asked, his mouth falling open.

Bismark puffed out his chest. "*Absolument!*" he confirmed, raising his chin toward the stars.

Dawn sighed knowingly.

"Well," stammered the sugar glider, pawing his fur, "what I meant to say is…wrestling is a strong word, of course…"

"But it was so big!" said Tobin, his eyes widening.

"Yes!" cried Bismark. "Humongous! Gigantic! Gargantuan! Unfathomably—"Catching sight of Dawn's frown, the sugar glider's words caught in his throat.

But the pangolin pressed on. "Were you injured?" he asked.

"Oh yes," replied Bismark. "You should've seen all the—"

Dawn cleared her throat.

"I mean...n-not quite," the sugar glider stammered, remembering the already-shed skin he'd encountered on his peaceful, moonlit stroll. "There was no...but yes! No! I mean...of course, yes! No! Collywobbles...polyglot...nincompoop... onomatopoeia!" Bismark's eyes rolled back in his head, as if searching the surface of his brain for more words.

"Eeeeeeee!" A bloodcurdling shriek interrupted Bismark's rant. It pierced the air and echoed, haunting and faint, through the trees.

"What was that?" cried Tobin, jumping behind the fox's raised tail.

Bismark crouched under his cape.

Even the fox seemed alarmed. Though her stance remained tall and brave, the hair on her back stood on end, like a long row of blades.

With vigilant eyes, she scanned the trees above. A curtain of drifting clouds obscured the moon, and the night's light shifted from a clear, deep blue to an ominous gray. She drew in her breath. "It appears the Brigade might be needed sooner than we had thought."

Chapter Two
TROUBLE BELOW

Dawn, Bismark, and Tobin listened closely, paws cupped to their ears. For a moment, all they could hear was the soft rush of the nearby river and the familiar buzzes and chirps of the night. Suddenly, there was another pained, desperate cry, followed by a scuffle, a thump, and a long, muffled wail. Then all fell silent. Eerily silent.

Dawn's ears remained pricked in attention. She scanned the land. Fixing her gaze on a tall nearby acacia, the fox straightened her spine. "Bismark," she said, "could you climb to the top of this tree? We should be able to see what's going on from up there."

"*Ma cherie*," he replied, puffing his chest. "Does a spring rain cleanse the soul? Does a dove's song fill the heart? Does the beautiful fox before me ignite every fiber of my being?"

Dawn waited.

"In a flash!" said the sugar glider.

Seconds later, Bismark stood on one of the tree's highest branches. He gazed at the river below. "Great Scott, I am handsome!" he said, marveling at his reflection.

Spotting a low-hanging limb, Dawn leapt off the ground, hoping she, too, could see more from a higher perch. At first she saw nothing unusual, just the froth of the river's current and the soft flicker of moonlight on the waves. But then she spotted a long, dark mass, blundering downstream toward them. "What is that?" she wondered.

Quickly, Tobin clambered up the tree's bark and settled, breathless, next to the fox.

"What do you see, *ma cherie*?" asked Bismark.

Dawn extended her neck. "I'm not sure."

Tobin looked at his friend with wide, hopeful

eyes. "Is it only a log?" he asked.

Dawn nodded. "Perhaps." She sat back on her haunches, a little less tense.

"Perhaps is good enough for *moi*!" said the sugar glider. "You worry too much, my lovely Dawn. The forest is full of screeches and howls. It is the music of the night. No *problemo* here!"

"Um… excuse me," started Tobin, self-consciously shifting his weight. "But it seems like we might have a… um… *'problemo*,' indeed!" The pangolin raised his brows in concern and motioned back toward the river.

The dark mass floated past beneath the tree, revealing itself to be an ordinary log—small leafless branches and coarse bark. However, clinging to the log's hollowed end was the distinct silhouette of a small, furry creature and the flash of its two terror-filled eyes.

"That animal is in trouble," Dawn whispered.

"Yes," Tobin nodded. The current had picked up now, and the creature was frantically splashing downstream.

"Well then," said Bismark, "I shall bid you *adieu*!"

"Excuse me?" said Tobin, tilting his chin toward his friend.

25

"Since I am the bravest soul of us all," said the sugar glider, "I shall gallantly remain in this tree—in its precarious limbs, at its most perilous pinnacle—while the two of you resolve that, um, teensy trouble down below." He cleared his throat and stood tall. "Faretheewell!"

"Oh," said the pangolin, sighing deeply in disappointment. "I suppose I thought a brigade did things together."

Dawn kept her eyes fixed on the river below, but her voice was clear and strong: "That's right, Tobin. We are a brigade. We will work as a team." She shot Bismark a commanding look. "Now, we must hurry! The river current is swift." She leapt to the ground and raced toward the riverbank.

"We're coming!" cried Tobin, scrambling headfirst down the tree.

"Indeed!" called the sugar glider. "We are right behind you, my dame!" Bismark stepped to the edge of the branch and directed himself toward Dawn's fluffy, white tail. He sighed. "The things I will do for this lady fox!" Bismark blew a kiss into the wind, spread his winglike flaps, and launched himself after his friends.

Chapter Three
THE SEARCH BEGINS

As the river picked up in speed, so did the Brigade. Dawn stayed in the lead, matching the current's pace. Bismark shadowed them from the treetops above, gliding from branch to branch. And Tobin trundled behind Dawn, trying his best to keep up.

"Oomph!" The pangolin winced as he stumbled over a pointy rock. Taking a seat on the long, damp grass, Tobin examined his tender foot and inspected his scales for nicks. "Oh dear," he muttered, noticing one on his leg. But then he noticed something moving in the aldrovanda bush just a tail's length away.

Tobin quietly rose to his feet and squinted into the brush.

"Hello?" he called, nervously coiling his tail. "Is somebody there?"

The pangolin padded closer and peered into the feathery leaves. There, tucked behind a cluster of deep scarlet blooms, he saw a quivering mound of fur and two terrified eyes.

"Oh," said Tobin, lowering his scaly head. "Hello."

Slowly, a fuzzy brown nose poked out of the brush. It wriggled twice and then retreated back into safety.

Suspecting the nose needed time to adjust, Tobin waited.

Sure enough, moments later, the nose reappeared. This time, a tentative paw followed. Little by little, one limb at a time, a stout, furry wombat emerged from the foliage, drenched and dripping with river water.

At once, the pangolin recognized those eyes— they were the same ones he had seen looking up from the log in terror. "Are you all right?" he asked, cocking his head.

But the wombat could not seem to reply. Despite the warmth of the night, her body trembled, from her round, fluffy cheeks to her short, stubby tail.

The pangolin scanned his surroundings for signs of Bismark or Dawn, but all he could see was the black of the night and the reflection of stars on the water. Not quite sure what to do, Tobin decided to simply introduce himself.

"My name is Tobin," he said, his voice soft and sincere.

Finally, the wombat spoke. "My name is Cora," she whispered. But still, she continued to shake, and her eyes remained frightened and wide.

Tobin cupped his scaled chin in his paw, searching for the right thing to say.

"When I'm afraid," he began, taking a seat on the ground, "I spray a smell from my scent glands. It can be rather unpleasant." Tobin bent his head in embarrassment. "And sometimes," he added, "I do it by accident, when there's nothing scary at all."

Cora nodded. "When I'm afraid, my fur quivers." She paused and drew in a deep breath. "But when I'm really afraid," she revealed, "I quiver on the inside." Cora wrapped her paws around her waist and looked out into the midnight sky.

Tobin looked out as well, but he was not sure for what. Then he remembered his friends. "I have a brigade," he told Cora, showcasing his shimmering cape.

Cora tilted her head. "What's a brigade?" she asked.

Tobin thought for a minute. "It's company," he proclaimed. "With matching outfits." Satisfied with his explanation, the pangolin smoothed a bit of snakeskin that had caught on his scales. "Would you like to meet them?" he asked.

For the first time that night, Cora's shoulders relaxed and the crease in her brow seemed to fade. She nodded.

But before Tobin could figure out which way to go, a familiar voice filled the air.

"Botanical beasts! Plants of pestilence! Villainous vines! Stand down, at once!" And then, just a short ways downstream, Bismark emerged, hacking the brush with a stick.

Tobin cleared his throat.

"Oh!" said the sugar glider, raising his chin. "It's you, my scale-skinned chum." Bismark pranced forward, still waving his stick through the air. "And, ooh!" he continued, spotting the wombat. "You've found yourself a little *amiga*!" He patted Tobin on the back. "I'm rubbing off on you already, I see." But then Bismark squinted and took a step back. "Why...it is you, *mademoiselle*! The damsel in such distress on the log." Bismark planted his twig machete into the ground. "Allow me to introduce myself: I am Bismark, god amongst gliders. And I am here to save you." The sugar glider graciously bowed.

Cora looked to Tobin.

"Come, these plants are not to be trusted— we must move to safety at once!" Bismark continued, wielding his twig again. "And that would be east, or west, or...I mean..." The sugar glider scratched the small patch of bald skin on the crown of his head.

"I believe we are safe right here," Dawn announced, as she, too, emerged from the brush. "I have searched the banks in both directions. Nothing seems out of the ordinary." The tawny fox crossed the grass to join the rest of the group.

"Dawn," said Tobin, "this is Cora."

"Cora," said Dawn, eying the wet, wide-eyed wombat, "did you just come from the river?"

Cora nodded.

Noticing that Cora was trembling again, the pangolin drew close to her side.

"Was that you we heard screaming? Are you in

some kind of trouble?" Dawn pressed.

The wombat looked at Tobin, who gave a reassuring tilt of his scales.

Cora drew in a deep breath. "My brother," she cried, the words coming at last. "My brother, Joe. He's... he's been taken!"

Dawn narrowed her eyes. "Taken by whom?" she asked.

The wombat shook her head from side to side. "I didn't see," she replied. "It all happened too fast. We were just chewing on roots." Cora gulped. "And then, all of a sudden, there was a noise...a rustling... then footsteps. My brother yelled at me to run, so I did, and...and..."

"And you didn't see who it was," confirmed Dawn.

Cora shook her head again. "We ran as fast as we could and jumped into the river." The wombat gazed toward the water. "I thought we'd be safe on the logs... but when I looked back, Joe was gone!"

Bismark let out a grunt. "We'll find the scoundrel who did this diabolical deed!" he snarled, tightening his grip on his stick.

Cora nodded in reply, but tears welled in her eyes and her brown fur continued to shake.

Tenderly, Tobin reached for her paw. "And your brother," he said. "We'll find him, too."

The fox gazed into the night. The moon had reemerged from the clouds and its glow was yellow and dim. She tried to shut out the thought that Cora's brother might have met a different, darker fate. "Yes," she said. "We will find him."

Chapter Four
THE NEW ARRIVALS

"It is mystifying! Stupefying! Absolutely flabbergastefying!" exclaimed Bismark, searching under a stone. "Where could your brother have gone?"

The animals were retracing their path up the river, looking for clues—footprints, torn branches, scratch marks on bark. Anything that might help them find Cora's brother.

"If only I had been there when you were being chased," said Bismark, stretching his flaps at full length. "I would've...I would've..." He paused, racking his brain. "Well," he continued, "I would've done something courageous, something grand, something très *magnifique!*"

"Cora," said Dawn, ignoring her friend, "do you think you would recognize the exact place where you jumped into the water? Or the last place you saw Joe?"

Cora was about to reply when suddenly, out of the midnight shadows, four rumpled bats barreled onto the scene, zigzagging out of control through the air.

"Look out!"

"Aye!"

"Ouch!"

"*Oy vey!*"

Wham! Splat! Smush! Crunch!

One after the other, the bats pummeled headfirst into the trunk of a tree, then landed in a mangled heap at its base.

"Oh goodness!" exclaimed Tobin. The pangolin cocked his head in concern at the mound of sinewy limbs and black wings.

"Excuse us!" said a bat, making his way to his feet.

"Just a small glitch in the biosonar," said another. "Perfectly normal."

Tobin stared with wide eyes. "Perfectly normal?" he asked.

The Brigade and the wombat eyed the bats as they rose to their feet, dusted their wings, and teetered into an unsteady line.

"Bats," muttered the sugar glider. "Absolutely disgusting."

The fox glared at Bismark. But upon inspecting the creatures before her, she understood what he meant. The fur on their chests was matted and mangy, and their rickety wings were covered in scrapes.

"Hmmm," Tobin mused. Squinting, he examined the bats then turned to Bismark. At a glance, the animals looked nearly identical. They were similar in size, with furless wings and fuzzy torsos. The pangolin blinked— his vision was always a little fuzzy. "Are you all related?"

The sugar glider gasped in horror. "No!" he exclaimed. "*Absolument* pas!" Bismark puffed out his chest. "I am a proud marsupial, not some cave-dwelling, ceiling-hanging rodent." The sugar glider spun on his toes, showcasing the black stripe on his back.

"Definitely a marsupial," muttered a bat.

"No ability to fly," said another.

Bismark's face flamed with rage. "Of course I can fly!" he yelled, flailing his flaps through the air.

"I glide through the tallest of trees. Soar through the windiest of winds. Sail through the stormiest of skies!"

"Glide? Yes."

"Soar? Maybe."

"Fly? No."

The bats huddled and snickered.

Dawn quickly stepped in to ease the tension. "Maybe you can help us," she said.

The creatures wobbled back into line.

"This is Cora," continued the fox, "and her brother is missing. Did you see any wombats as you flew past?"

"Can't much see," said a bat.

"Terrible eyes," said another.

"That's why we use echolocation," explained a third. "We send out a sound, it hits something, then it echoes back. That's how we locate the object."

"Though that's on the fritz, too," said the fourth. He rubbed his throat. "Larynx trouble."

Dawn paused, a bit confused now herself. "So… you don't know of any strange occurrences?"

"Strange occurrences?"

"We know all about those."

"Terrible mess in the valley these days!"

"Animals disappearing faster than tsetse flies on the tongue!"

The bats all answered in turn.

"You mean, you know of others who have recently vanished?" The fur on Dawn's back stood on end.

"*Svor*! Never seen these parts so empty."

"Nor so quiet."

"Except for the screams...."

The fox's breath caught in her throat. The bats had confirmed her fear that Cora's brother had not disappeared just by chance. He was one victim of many. And there would be many more if the Brigade did not intervene.

Chapter Five
THE CREATURE

"I must face the truth, feel the blow, suffer the pain!" Bismark wailed as he paced amidst the tall grass. Bismark was still agitated as he rose from his bed in time to see the first evening star. After the encounter with those four irksome creatures, he had slept terribly.

"You do not look like a bat!" insisted Tobin.

The pangolin tumbled out from the hollow eucalyptus where he had slept. He felt terrible. He had not meant to offend the small sugar glider the previous evening—not at all. But Bismark ignored the pangolin and turned instead to the fox.

"Dawn, I beg of you. The truth. I must have it!" Dramatically, the sugar glider fell to his knees, clasping his fingers as if in prayer.

"Bismark." Dawn sighed. "You do not look like a bat."

"Really? Do you mean it?" Bismark glanced up at the fox, his eyes full of hope.

"Goodness, no!" Tobin quickly chimed in. "Not at all!"

"Dawn, can you gaze upon my face without the image of a blood-sucking rodent entering your mind?"

"Bismark, enough," said the fox. "You are very handsome. And you do not look like a bat."

"Of course I don't!" he exclaimed, bounding back to his feet. "Do you see the sheen of this fur? The elegant curve of this tail? The strong line of this jaw? A bat? Impossible!"

The little sugar glider rushed to the fox, threw his arms around her shins, and buried his face in her fur. "Oh, my beloved!" he cried. "I thank you. I thank you for your honesty and your clear vision." Bismark gave a deep, grateful bow.

Tobin smiled. But then, as Cora emerged from the eucalyptus, his forehead creased with concern. The wombat, sweaty, sleepy, and shaky, had clearly suffered fitful dreams.

"Maybe we should get going soon," offered the pangolin.

"Yes," Dawn agreed. She walked over to the bats, who were just waking as well. "Make sure to have a drink before we set out. It might be a long march."

"Good thinking, fox," said a bat.

"The old gullet was getting a bit parched," agreed his brother.

"*Svor.*"

Tobin and Cora also leaned over the bank and took a few sips of river water, but Bismark turned toward the fox. "Did you know," he began, "that sugar gliders need less water than bats? We can survive on just a few raindrops a day." Beaming with pride, Bismark reclined against a small rock and plucked a leaf from a fern. "True fact," he continued, licking a droplet of dew from the plant. "That, *mio amore*, is just one of the many ways the sugar glider outshines the bat, though I am happy to share all the others." He cleared his throat, stood, and mounted the rock. "Shall we begin with where it begins?" he said. "Birth."

Bismark raised a stick in the air in preparation for his lecture. But before he could speak, the midnight sky rang with a sudden, loud scream.

"Eeeeeeee!"

Snap!

Boom!

The forest shook, branches broke, and something heavy fell with a thud.

"*Mon dieu!*" cried Bismark, crouching behind his stone.

"Oh goodness!" Tobin gulped. "What was that?"

"That was the same noise I heard last night when Joe disappeared!" Cora piped up.

"Aye!"

"*Svor!*"

"That's the one!" the bats confirmed.

"Quick," the fox commanded. "Follow me." Dawn bolted upstream toward the sound. Cora, Bismark, and Tobin quickly followed, running full-speed. The bats scrambled to bring up the rear. Suddenly, the wombat called out, "Stop!"

The group came to a halt.

"Here," Cora breathed. "It was here. I remember because of those rocks."

Dawn, Tobin, and the wombat inspected the jagged formation jutting into the river. Bismark glided close behind.

"I detect traces of a struggle," Dawn remarked.

"Wombat hairs, nail scratches in the moss—thankfully, there are no signs that someone was eaten."

Cora sighed with relief.

"But it's strange," Dawn continued. "There's no trail leading to or away from here. It's as if Joe simply disappeared."

Dawn and Cora circled the rocks, searching for clues. Bismark followed Dawn, purely for the sake of it, and the bats poked around in the riverbank. Tobin lingered back near the tree line. His keen ears detected a twig snapping in the bushes behind them. With the others distracted, the pangolin decided to investigate the sound himself.

Cautiously, Tobin peered into the dense tangle of leaves. At first, he couldn't make out much of anything besides dark branches and shadows. But then he caught a glimpse of two small points of light. He squinted, trying to see a little more clearly. Were those berries catching the moonlight? Perhaps drops of dew?

As suddenly as the lights appeared, they winked out. Tobin leaned in closer, tilting his head to the side, hoping to see them again.

There they were! But this time, they were larger, closer. Two deep, brown rings with dark dots at the centers. Eyes! Someone was watching them.

Chapter Six
THE SCOUTS

"Oh dear!" cried Tobin. "Everyone, come quick!"

In an instant, Dawn, Bismark, Cora, and the bats appeared at his side.

"There's an animal in there!" Tobin whispered, pointing to the dense brush.

Together, the four friends and the bats formed a line and slowly stepped toward the bush. They craned their heads forward. Something was moving in there, but it was too fast to track.

"Tobin, what did you see?" asked Dawn.

As if in response, two large ears popped up from the grass nearby, followed by a long tail with a brush-like tuft of fur at the end. The body of the creature was hidden as it sprinted away into the forest.

Her teeth bared, the fox pounced after the creature. The hair on her back stood up in wiry spikes.

"Be careful, *mia bella*!" cried Bismark, clasping his heart with both hands.

But Dawn was too late. The mysterious animal had disappeared into the dark woods.

"Everyone, stay on guard," said the fox. She had no doubt that the creature was hiding nearby, watching them still. Her eyes darted over the brush, searching for any sign of the long-tailed spy. "And if anyone sees or hears something unusual, give the following call." Dawn raised her head and yowled a high-pitched note.

The others nodded.

"Like this?" asked Cora. "*Arooo.*"

"No time to be shy!" declared Bismark. "A real howl is born from the gut. Now listen and learn." The sugar glider took a deep breath, closed his eyes, and yodeled into the night.

"Yes," said the bats. "With *chutzpah*!"

"Blurghhhh," Tobin gurgled.

"No, no, no," said the sugar glider. "Much too much throat."

"Blurghhhh!" The pangolin continued to gurgle. He was growing red in the face.

Cora looked at her friend with concern. "Are you okay?" she asked.

"The call!" said Tobin. "I'm making the call. Look!" The pangolin pointed toward the tree line ahead. Waddling out of the leaves were two flightless birds. With their fuzzy brown feathers and little round bodies, they resembled a pair of coconuts.

"Plump prowlers of the night!" yelled the sugar glider. "Explain your presence at once!"

The birds bumbled toward the group.

"My name is Burt," said the smaller of the two. "And this here is Becka, my wife. We were simply searching for food."

"Humph!" exclaimed Bismark. "Searching for victims, more like it!"

The fox shook her head at the sugar glider's distrust. It was clear that these kiwi birds posed no threat. "I apologize," she said, speaking on her friend's behalf.

"Oh, it's okay," said Becka. "Everyone seems on

edge in these dangerous times."

Dawn's ears stood erect. "Dangerous times?"

"Oh, yes," replied Burt. "Terrible, these nappings. Just terrible."

Cora stepped forward, eyes wide. "Nappings? You know of them, too?"

The kiwi birds nodded. "How could we not?" replied Burt. "Seems like everywhere you go, animals are missing."

Becka nodded. "Twenty-two years, we've been together. Twenty-two years, and twenty-two tots. Chose this place for the kids. A family area, a peaceful place. And now…" Tearfully, she buried her beak in Burt's feathered breast. "Well, I'm just worried sick!"

"There, there, Peaches. There, there," whispered Burt. "You just let it all out." Tenderly, the bird stroked his wife's head. Then he turned back toward the Brigade. "We've lost so many," he said. "So many dear friends."

"Twelve," said Becka, raising her face from Burt's chest. "Just last night, my cousin Bailey was taken!" The kiwi burst into sobs.

Burt lowered his feathered head. "You're down at Patterson Pond, minding your own business, looking for worms in the mud," he sighed. "And the next thing you know…whomp! Gone."

The wombat groaned, and scrunched her eyes shut. Tobin rested his paw on her shoulder.

"Wait," said Dawn, approaching the birds. "What was that you just said?"

Burt looked in her eyes. "Whomp!" he repeated, this time with more force.

"No, no," muttered Dawn. "The other thing. About the pond."

"Oh!" said Burt, clearing his throat. "Right. Yes. Like I said, poor Bailey was just down by Patterson Pond. You know, the one near the coyote dens. That's where all the plump worms live." The kiwi bowed his head. "Those delicious, delicious worms."

"Tragic," said Becka. "Digging in the mud one minute, disappeared the next. Absolutely tragic."

"Tragic, yes," said Dawn, but the fox looked preoccupied. As if pulled by an invisible string, she was drawn toward the river. The others followed.

"What is it?" Tobin asked, joining the fox.

"Patterson Pond," she said. She stared at the opposite bank, lost completely in her thoughts.

A cool breeze blew through the grass, sending a chill down Tobin's spine.

Dawn turned back toward the birds. "Why don't you two go check on your children?" she said. "Thank you for sharing your story. You've been very helpful."

The kiwis nodded and then, side-by-side, shuffled back toward the woods.

Dawn looked at Bismark, Tobin, and Cora. Her Brigade-mates stared back at her, waiting for instruction.

"We must cross the river," she said, her voice determined and strong, "and make our way toward the pond."

"Toward the pond?" said Bismark. "You mean, toward the coyotes!" His eyes bulged out of his head. "Have you gone *loco*, my lady?"

Tobin shuddered. The coyotes were crafty, cruel killers with big appetites. But he knew they had to find Joe, and now the missing kiwi birds, too. "Let's go," he said, forcing himself to sound brave.

Everyone nodded. Although they were scared of what they might find across the river, something told them Dawn had a plan.

Chapter Seven
THE CROSSING

"Ah, Dawn," sighed Bismark. "Not only the name of our beautiful leader, but also the time when we night prowlers should be asleep!" The sugar glider yawned and plopped himself down on the ground. The morning sun was already beating down on them, baking the dry soil and making the air shimmer.

Dawn approached Bismark. "Stand up," she directed. "We can rest when we get to that pond."

"Rest? Or face certain death?" cried the sugar

glider. Reluctantly, he hoisted himself to his feet. "If we don't get nabbed on the way, we'll be gobbled by those nasty coyotes when we get there!"

Dawn turned back toward the river. "We must cross," she said, surveying the banks. "It is only a question of how."

"We could make a raft," said a bat.

The others flapped their leathery wings in agreement. "Most cunning! Most clever!"

"Most thickheaded," snapped Bismark. He turned to the bats. "Surely, you see the current moves far too fast for a floating device. We would be miles downstream before we reached the other side."

"I'm afraid he's correct," agreed Dawn. The fox lowered her face to the water and prodded at it with one outstretched paw.

"Animals of boundless flight," said the sugar glider, taunting the bats. "When will your sonar be fixed so you can find yourselves a good idea?"

Dawn ignored the bickering. "Look at these sea cucumbers." She pointed to the knobby cucumber-like creatures floating in the water. "They shouldn't be here."

"What do you mean?" Cora leaned over the water's edge, her brow creased with confusion.

"They are saltwater creatures," said Dawn.

"They should be in the sea, not the river."

Curious, the pangolin extended his exceptionally long tongue to investigate further. "Ick!" he exclaimed, quickly snapping it back.

"*Oy gevalt!*" gasped the bats. In unison, they extended their wings toward Tobin.

"That's not a tongue—"

"—that's a jump rope!"

The bats cackled.

"Oh goodness, yes," stammered the pangolin. "My tongue." Self-conscious, he covered his mouth with one paw.

"Enough," Dawn commanded. "Tobin, what's wrong with the water?"

"It tastes salty, I think. Just a little bit."

Dawn dipped a paw in the water and then licked it. "You're right," she confirmed.

"Most clever canine, illuminate this finding. Empower us with knowledge. Tell us what this means!" exclaimed Bismark.

"This means that, for some reason, sea water has mixed into this freshwater stream." Dawn looked out onto the river.

"So the sea cucumbers are lost," concluded Tobin.

"Yes," said the fox. Gently, she placed a paw onto one of the long blobs. It continued to float near the surface, supporting her weight surprisingly well. "Hmm," she said. "I think the sea cucumbers could be very helpful to us. If we could just think of a way to control their direction…"

But the bats were no longer listening. Bored of river talk, they had surrounded Tobin.

"Can it feel that?" asked one.

"Can it taste this?" said a second.

The pangolin yelped.

"What are you doing?" Dawn gasped. The fox turned to see all four bats prodding Tobin's stomach with their long bony fingers.

"Says he stores it right here," said a bat.

"It's longer than his body!" cried another.

"What's longer than his body?" asked Cora.

Tobin blushed. "My tongue," he replied, cradling his belly. "It coils in my stomach when I'm not using it." Slowly, the pangolin inched away from the bats in the direction of the fox. "Dawn!" he said, eager to change the subject. "They're going after that green stuff in the water." Indeed, slowly but surely, the sea cucumbers were chasing after the flecks of algae floating downstream.

The fox's face brightened. "Come," she said. Dawn searched the edge of the river, gathering green plants with her paws. "Collect all the algae you can and then store it in your mouths."

"I don't understand," said the wombat. "Should we eat it?"

"No. This is how we will cross the river," Dawn said, a green wad already tucked in her bottom lip. "Watch."

Chapter Eight
SEA CUCUMBER EXPRESS

The fox mounted the sea cucumbers, each paw on one blob. From her mouth, she sprinkled small bits of algae in front of her. Sure enough, the creatures started wriggling toward the food, taking Dawn along for the ride.

"It's working!" Tobin said. "They're moving across the river!" Eagerly, the pangolin mimicked Dawn's actions, climbing aboard the sea cucumbers and luring them forward with their favorite food.

Bismark and Cora soon followed. And so did the bats.

"What are you doing?" snapped the sugar glider. "You have wings! Can't you fly across?"

"Sonar still broken," said a bat.

"Why fly when you can ride?" asked another.

Bismark clenched his jaw. "Lazy bats," he muttered.

"Come now," said Dawn, calling over her shoulder. "The sooner we cross, the sooner we can find the missing animals."

Tobin nodded in agreement, and as he did, a large clump of algae dropped from his mouth to the water. His sea cucumbers shot toward the food. "Oh goodness!" he cried, speeding forward.

Cora giggled. "Wheee!" she exclaimed. "I can feel the wind in my fur!"

"It's a cucumber cavalry!" said the sugar glider.

"A speedy salad!" added Tobin.

"Hey, stop eating all the algae!" said one of the bats to his companion.

"I can't help it if these cucumbers have good taste in bait," said the bat, chewing down a mouthful of the slimy green matter.

"That's the last of it. I ate mine too," said another.

"I suppose we'll have to use wind power now."

The bats extended their wings, which caught the wind like sails. The foursome zoomed on ahead, passing the Brigade and Cora. Their steering, however, was wonky and soon—Bam! Oof! Plop!—they crashed into a rock and tumbled into the river.

As the Brigade stepped off their sea cucumbers onto the rocky bank, the bats pulled themselves onto the shore, dripping wet, fists raised in triumph.

"Made it," said one.

"Bit of an unexpected dip."

"Water up the nose, that's for sure."

"But sweet—cough, cough—glory."

Now on the other side of the river, Dawn peered through the trees. She could see the glittering surface of Patterson Pond. Sharp, distant howls warbled through the early morning air. The coyotes' den was not far.

Chapter Nine
THE WARNING CALL

"One, two, three!" chanted the bats. The march to the coyotes' den took them down a shadowy path through the heart of a gum tree forest. The animals were all tired—having had only a few hours of sleep.

"So much senseless chatter," grumbled Bismark. "These bats talk just to hear themselves speak!"

Dawn wasn't listening to the sugar glider's complaints. She was scanning their surroundings for any signs of movement in the darkness. Something didn't feel right. A westerly breeze blew in from the direction of the nearby pond, carrying with it a musty, sour scent.

"Oh goodness, is that what coyotes smell like?" asked Tobin. His scales were bunched together in fear.

A shrill howl rose up nearby and Bismark halted. "Wait! *Basta*! This is madness! We are about to walk into the jaws of these vicious predators! This goes against every instinct in my beautiful, bite-free body!"

"I'm certain Dawn has a plan to keep us safe, Bismark," said Tobin.

"My lovely fox," said the sugar glider, "enlighten us as to the specifics of this plan of yours. Will my role involve being chewed, swallowed, or otherwise eaten?"

Dawn opened her mouth to respond but then suddenly stopped. She squinted, raised her head, and let out a quiet yowl.

"I see that I have moved you beyond what words can express," said Bismark. He blew on his nails casually. "I was not even trying, you know."

Dawn shook her head then made the sound again.

"Oh goodness, does your stomach hurt? I think I swallowed a bit too much of that algae, myself," said the pangolin.

Dawn sighed. "The distress call was a bad idea. From now on, let's just say 'help,' or 'look over there'."

Bismark nodded. "Yes, no need to speak in nonsensical sounds that nobody can really understand, *ça va?*"

"So, look over there," whispered Dawn. She bobbed her neck in the direction of some tall grass by the side of the path. At first glance, it was perfectly ordinary, except for an odd flower with a long, drooping stalk and a blossom like a paintbrush. But there, between the blades of grass, were two familiar points of light.

"Oh goodness," Tobin whispered.

"Don't be alarmed, my innocent friend," Bismark said to Tobin. "The fox is merely drawing our attention to the beautiful scenery. What are these spooky-looking trees called, my love?"

There was no reply. Bismark's brow furrowed. All seven animals—Dawn, Tobin, Cora, and the four bats—gazed past him, their eyes trained on something just behind him. And they all wore expressions of fear. "*Mon dieu*! Is it something I said?" asked the sugar glider, his eyes growing wide.

Cora shook her head.

Slowly, Bismark rotated his head and looked over his shoulder.

"Ahhhh!" Spotting the eyes of the spy, the sugar glider shrieked.

"Eeeek!" So did the strange little creature.

"Ohhh!" The rest of the crew replied. And then they sprang into action.

Tobin shot a noxious scent from his gland. Bismark lunged forward, his gliding flaps spread wide. Dawn pounced with bared teeth.

There was a great commotion as a flurry of dirt and dust surrounded the animals. There were shouts here, furry limbs there, a bundle of bat wings flapping—chaos. When the uproar subsided and the air cleared, the animals saw the suspect before them, pinned and writhing beneath the commanding paws of the fox.

Chapter Ten
THE JERBOA

"**D**-d-d-don't hurt me!" stammered the creature, trembling with fear beneath Dawn's sturdy paw. "P-please! Let me go!"

"Pah!" scoffed Bismark, placing his hands on his hips. "Do not liberate that dangerous beast!"

Dawn kept her paw firmly planted. She needed no advice.

"D-d-dangerous?" echoed the animal. "That's impossible! I'm t-t-t-tiny!"

Tobin squinted. The creature was indeed tiny. From his head to his haunches, he was only half the size of the sugar glider. In fact, with his oversized ears, puny body, and long tail, he looked like a miniature, malnourished mouse—hardly the profile of an animal napper. But still, there was something strained about the way he spoke that made the pangolin suspicious.

"P-p-please," begged the creature. He sniveled and coughed. "My t-t-tail. Look out for my tail!" Nervously, he eyed Dawn's rear paw. "It's very s-s-sensitive."

But the fox still did not move. "Bring me something to tie him," she instructed the bats. "We will secure this stranger until we know more."

"Right away!" said the bats. They stripped the surrounding greenery and quickly wove together a cord out of stalks and vines.

With the creature restrained, Dawn finally lifted her paw. "Who are you?" she asked, leaning in. Her eyes narrowed to slivers.

"I'm J-J-Jerry," he said, tilting away from the fox. "J-J-Jerry the g-g-gentle jerboa." The animal delivered a shaky smile that strained his cheeks and jaw.

Not convinced, Dawn leaned in even closer. "Can you tell us anything about a missing wombat?"

"And kiwis," added Tobin.

"Oh, k-kiwi," said Jerry. "I love kiwi. Delicious and high in water c-c-c-content. The seeds g-g-get stuck in my teeth, though."

"Not the fruit!" snapped a bat.

"The bird," said another.

Dawn locked eyes with the jerboa. "We are investigating a wave of animal disappearances," she said. "Do you have any information?"

Jerry squirmed in his bonds. "I c-c-can't think," he sputtered. "These v-v-vines are c-c-cutting off my circulation."

With a sigh, the fox motioned for the bats to loosen the rope.

"M-m-much better," said the jerboa. The animal stretched and rose to his feet.

Cora let out a gasp. "His legs," she whispered, drawing close to Tobin.

The pangolin nodded. The creature had long hind legs, spindly and bent backwards at the knee, like a flamingo's.

"L-l-l-let me think," he stalled, shifty eyes darting from one animal to the next. "W-w-well," he continued, "I h-h-have heard a good deal of c-c-c-commotion recently...."

Dawn glared at the creature. "Out with it," she demanded.

"Don't play *stupido*!" Bismark chimed in. "We saw you at the scene of the crime. Practically caught you red-pawed!"

"R-r-right," stammered Jerry, a bit flustered now.

Cora stepped toward him, tears misting her eyes. "Please," she begged.

Tobin padded to his wombat friend's side. "Her brother was taken," he explained. "Is there anything you know that could help us?"

"I don't know anything! I s-s-swear!" stammered Jerry.

"Then why were you down by the river?" pressed Dawn. "We saw you watching us from the bushes."

Jerry eyes darted to the ground. "I was h-hiding," he said. "I was so s-s-scared." "My family was taken, too," he muttered. "I thought maybe y-y-you were the n-n-nappers."

Bismark placed his hands on his hips. "Tell us more! Give us evidence of your innocence!" he demanded, flashing his cape. "*Pronto!*"

"Prong toe?" asked the creature, scrunching his nose in confusion.

"No!" said the sugar glider. "'*Pronto.*' It means, 'hurry up and tell us what you know'!"

"I'm sorry," said Jerry, twiddling his paws. "I have a hard t-t-time understanding all you b-b-bats."

"For the last time!" wailed Bismark, clenching his fists. The sugar glider spun around, showcasing his long furry tail. "I am none other than Animalia, Chordata, Mammalia, MAR-SUP-IALIA!"

"He's not a bat," Tobin said, translating the rant.

"Not at all," agreed Cora.

"Marsupial," muttered the bats. "Definitely a marsupial."

"Jerry," said Dawn, undistracted, "if your family has been taken, will you join in our search? We need all the eyes and ears we can get."

All eyes bore down on the little rodent. His long tail twitched.

"Why y-y-yes," he stammered, "of course." The jerboa nervously shifted his weight. "Anything I can do to help."

Dawn studied the sky. The moon was on its way down to the horizon. "Let's go," she commanded, "while we still have some time before daybreak." She eyed the tiny creature. She did not trust the jerboa. She did not trust him at all.

Chapter Eleven
THE DARK DEN

"*On y va!*" said the sugar glider. "Off we go!"
Bismark spun on his toes then sidled alongside the
jerboa. "You, my pocket-sized picaroon, will walk with
me so I may educate you on the basics of taxonomy."
Jerry squinted at Bismark. "Is that another one of your
exotic l-l-languages?"

"Oh *mon dieu*." The sugar glider sighed. "You
have much to learn, puny pal. Much to learn."

The Brigade set out, Bismark and Jerry leading
the way, the others close behind.

"Taxonomy!" declared Bismark. "The way we name and identify the creatures of this world." He cleared his throat, ready to deliver another one of his lectures. "The order of things. Classification." He gave a whirl of his cape. "Naturally, sugar gliders are at the pinnacle, the peak, the tippiest of the top. Where you should start, perhaps, is the bottom—bats. Why don't you go ask them how they ended up in such a sorry state?"

Bismark gave the jerboa a gentle push toward the chattering bats. Then he fell back a few paces to confer with Tobin.

"I think he's a resourceful rodent. A fine fellow. A jolly good chap!" he said, elbowing the pangolin.
"Yes." Tobin nodded, though his face crumpled in disagreement.

"I must admit," continued the sugar glider, "I wasn't so sure about the jerboa at first. But now, I agree. He's a fine addition to the search party! Plus," he continued, scratching his bald patch absentmindedly, "one should never be criticized for diminutive size."

"Oh no!" said Tobin. "Not at all."

"What are you two discussing?" asked Dawn. The nimble fox glided up to her friends, keeping an eye on the jerboa.

"Just reviewing the character of our new acquaintance," replied Bismark. "A good chap, that Jerry."

Dawn gazed up ahead. Cora and the bats were gathered around the jerboa. "Tobin," said the fox, "what do you think?"

The pangolin shrugged his scales. "Um, well," he said.

"Yes?" pressed Dawn.

"Well…" he began again. "Yes. He's a good chap." But the pangolin's answer was hesitant.

Her brow creased with concern, Dawn looked carefully at the jerboa. Jerry was shuffling forward with his peculiar hopping gait, and the bats were clumsily mimicking his movements behind him.

"Excuse me?" Cora joined them, her soft voice edged with panic. "But I was wondering, do any of you hear that noise?"

Tobin cocked his head to the wind. He heard howling nearby. "Oh goodness," he uttered. "Are those…?"

"Coyotes," Dawn finished.

The fox let out a breath. "Enough fooling around now," she commanded the bats, who were still aping the jerboa's walk. "Let's walk in formation. We can't have anyone too far ahead of or behind the group."

With Jerry still in loose holds, the nine nocturnals threaded their way through the shaded wood. After some time, Dawn stopped and motioned for the others to gather.

"The coyote den is just ahead," she announced. "We must approach it with caution."

"Approach?" balked the sugar glider. His bulbous eyes seemed to pop from his head. "When you say approach, do you mean what I think you mean? As in, get close to? Go near? Walk toward?"

"The coyotes have lived here long, and they know the land well," explained Dawn. "They might be able to help in our quest." The fox gazed into the depths of the wood.

"Or devour us!" Bismark wiped beads of sweat from his brow with his paw.

"Scared."

"Trembling."

"Definitely nervous."

The bats all agreed, evaluating the sugar glider.

Dawn sighed. "Perhaps it is best that I go alone," she resolved.

"What's that, my lady?" The sugar glider leapt onto a rock. "You'd like me, the marsupial, to hold down the fort? To serve as our group's fearless leader whilst you are gone?"

Dawn, not really listening to the sugar glider, focused on the dark wood ahead.

Tobin padded to his friend's side. "I don't like the idea of you going alone," he said softly. "I'll come with you."

"Very well." The fox smiled at her loyal Brigade-mate. Then she turned toward the others. "Be alert," she advised. Dawn scanned the group. Her gaze lingered on Jerry. "We do not know what dangers surround us."

Chapter Twelve
THE WRITING ON THE WALL

Dawn and Tobin crept across a meadow, making sure to stay low in the tall grass. As they approached the side of a small hill, Dawn slowed. There before them was a deep, dark hole nestled between large slabs of gray rock. The coyote den.

Dawn lifted a paw but then paused.

"Are you okay?" asked Tobin.

The fox drew in a long breath. "Yes," she said. "I'm all right."

Tobin nodded, but something in the tone of Dawn's voice made him think there was more she was not saying.

"Let's move on." Dawn lengthened her neck, placed her paw on the ground, and proceeded to the den's mouth. Lingering at the threshold, she and the pangolin peered into the dark.

"Look," said Tobin. Although his eyesight was poor, he had spotted strange markings on the dirt-covered walls.

The fox crawled deeper into the cave and examined the drawings. Though at a distance they seemed to be nothing more than muddy paw prints, upon closer inspection the smudges and smears proved to represent various animals—including raccoons, kiwis, and a wombat.

"Hieroglyphics," Dawn murmured.

"Oh goodness, oh goodness!" sputtered the pangolin, nervously backing away. "Some of these animals are the ones who are missing!"

"Tobin," warned Dawn, "do not jump to conclusions." Tobin gulped. His friend was acting strangely defensive.

"Oh, um, I'm sorry," he stammered. "But I'm not sure this is safe." Tobin's voice was shaking now, and his scales trembled with fear.

"The pangolin is right." A deep voice echoed through the den. "It is not safe for you here."

At once, Dawn jumped with alarm, and Tobin's eyes bulged wide. Together, they turned around. A giant, pale gray coyote was standing at the mouth of the den. With his long legs and broad chest, he appeared twice the size of the two others combined.

Tobin's heart lurched and his breath caught in his throat. He furled his scales for protection and tried to steady himself. His feet felt as if they belonged to someone else.

Dawn, however, did not seem scared at all. Her back fell from its arch, her muscles relaxed, and her face grew soft.

Tobin gaped at his friend. With a giant coyote staring them down, Dawn somehow grew calmer, more relaxed.

"Yes," said the fox, her voice even and strong. "We know it's not safe. What we don't know is why."

The coyote stared at the fox. "It's been a long time," he said.

"It has," replied Dawn. Her whiskers twitched.

For a moment, the two canines stood still, eyes locked. The coyote's coarse hair billowed in the cool evening breeze. Dawn's tail flicked from left to right. Although they were silent, the air between them seemed full of unspoken words.

The pangolin bowed his head. His heart continued to race, but he knew there was nothing to fear.

A chorus of low howls rang in the distance, shattering the stillness of the moment. The coyote turned his broad head toward the sound.

"You must go," he declared. "The pack is returning. You cannot be here when they arrive."

"But these images—" Dawn started.

"Not now," said the coyote, cutting her off. He paused. "Meet me at sunrise, at the glen to the north. Just beyond the dragon trees." The canine glanced at Tobin and then returned his gaze to the fox. "Come alone," he instructed.

And with that, the majestic coyote descended deeper into his den.

Dawn watched his silhouette melt into the darkness. But then, at the sound of the approaching pack, she turned and motioned for Tobin to follow. Hastily, the two animals moved through the night, retracing their path through the meadow and the tall grass. Once they were a safe distance away, they slowed and walked side by side.

Although Tobin had many questions, he remained quiet and waited for his friend to speak.

"That was Ciro," Dawn said at last. "He is the leader of the coyotes in the eastern regions."

Tobin waited for more.

"He will have information about the nappings. I will meet him at sunrise, as he requested." Her voice dropped to a whisper, as though she spoke to herself. Her eyes flashed in the light of the moon. "This time, I must go alone."

Chapter Thirteen
THE WAIT

"It is most confusing! *Muy* befuddling! *Absolument* absurd!" Bismark ranted and swung a stick through the air. The sun was rising, and there was no sign of Dawn.

"Calm down!"

"Sit tight."

"The canine calls the shots."

"*Svor*! The canine—"

But Bismark cut off the fourth bat. "*Mon dieu!*" he fumed, wringing his tiny fists. "Must you always speak in sequence? It's like talking to a bell. Ding, dang, dong!" The sugar glider grunted, pacing back and forth. "Now I know the true meaning of 'dingbat'."

Bismark slouched in despair and gazed into the brush. Dawn had vanished into the leaves quite some time ago. "I just don't understand," he whimpered. "Why does she want us to wait here? Is this some sort of test? Some kind of game?"

Tobin fidgeted and pawed at his scales. He, too, was waiting.

"Come now, pangolin," pressed Bismark. "You were with her. You must know something!"

"Yes," said Cora, padding up to Tobin. "Are you sure you saw nothing unusual?"

"Oh! Oh goodness, no," Tobin fibbed. "Just the coyote den." The pangolin did not like to lie—he didn't even really know how. But he had a deep sense that Dawn would want him to keep what he knew to himself. She had, after all, explained next to nothing about what had happened between her and that coyote, Ciro.

Sensing that Tobin needed space, Cora shifted the focus to the jerboa. "Jerry," she said, "you've been awfully quiet. Is there anything else you can tell us?"

The jerboa clasped his hands and, once again, launched into his tale of woe.

Tobin smiled at Cora, grateful for the moment of peace. To clear his head, he left the group and climbed to the top of a nearby hill. Since his trip to the den, he'd felt quite overwhelmed. Again, he replayed the events of the night in his mind. He had seen drawings of kiwis and a wombat—animals they knew to be missing. But raccoons? A tarantula? And the others? There were a few sketches Tobin couldn't make out at the time. What did these pictures mean? Perhaps these nocturnal nappings were even more widespread than they thought.

"Tobin!" Bismark's shrill voice rang from downhill.

"Oh, um, yes?" said the pangolin, jarred from his thoughts. He waddled down to where Bismark and the others were gathered.

"Tell these dingbats of my natural leadership qualities." The sugar glider placed his hands on his hips and looked expectantly at his friend.

"He wants to be Acting Commander," explained Cora. "To take charge while Dawn is away." The wombat eyed Bismark with doubt.

"But we nominate you," said a bat.

"Yes, the scaly one!" said another.

Tobin's eyes widened. "Me?" he asked, drawing back.

"You see?" Bismark shouted, raising his arms in the air. "He is tentative! Hesitant! Not fit for command!" He glanced at Tobin. "No offense."

Tobin shrugged, too distracted to care. Dawn had been gone quite a while, and he was beginning to worry.

"Under my lead, we shall go on adventures! Brave the beyond! Find our dear fox!" Bismark waved his stick with each word.

The jerboa hopped forward. "That's a great idea." His eyes darted toward the woods. "Let's v-v-venture."

The pangolin gulped. He knew they should not depart from the ridge. With all the recent nappings, it was far too dangerous. Plus, he had to keep Dawn's whereabouts private—Ciro had specifically asked to meet her alone. "Let's just stay here," he proposed. "Dawn will be back soon."

"*Oy vey.*"

"Not so great."

"Pains us to say it…"

"… but we side with the glider."

Tobin looked at the bats, yapping and flapping their wings. "Oh dear," he sighed, turning to Cora for help.

"I don't know," the wombat said. "What if Dawn is in trouble? What if she needs our help?"

Tobin's heart raced with desperation. Then he saw something moving along the horizon. Something with pointy ears, perfect posture, and glowing red fur.

"Oh goodness!" the pangolin uttered. "Look!"

"Dawn!" exclaimed Bismark. The sugar glider dropped the stick he'd been wielding and ran, arms spread, toward the fox. "Our champion, our hero, our savior!"

"Thank goodness, you're here!" added Cora.

"Yes, yes, *svor*," said the bats. "*Shalom*, welcome back, welcome back." The four animals stumbled in line and raised their wings in salute.

Dawn straightened her spine. "Members and friends of the Nocturnal Brigade, gather in. I have much to share."

Eagerly, the group drew toward the fox.

"Tonight," she continued, "I met with others who have been investigating these nappings. And I have formed an alliance." She paused. "From this point on, we shall band together with the coyotes."

There was a hiccup of silence…then an explosion of protest.

"Coyotes?" shrieked Bismark.

"Pitiless predators!"

"Howling hunters!"

"Blood-thirsty beasts!"

The bats' wings shook with worry. Cora and Tobin also looked nervous, and they huddled together in fear.

"The coyotes are not our enemies," declared Dawn. "But from what I have gathered, there is one among us whom we cannot trust...." The fox scanned the group. The hair on her spine rose on end. "Where is Jerry?" she gasped.

Bismark looked right and then left. Cora and Tobin spun in circles. The bats flapped their wings overhead.

"Oh goodness!" blurted the pangolin. "I don't know! He was here just a moment ago—"

"Find him!" cried Dawn.

At once, the animals scattered, searching for the wily jerboa. But after pawing through thickets and combing the low grassy hillside, it was clear that their hunt was hopeless. Jerry was gone.

Chapter Fourteen
THE ALLIANCE

"Oh *mon dieu!*" wailed the sugar glider. "It's the end of the road. The final act. Showdown at high moon!"

"There is nothing to be afraid of," said Dawn. "When we meet the coyotes, that will be clear."

"Clear that I'm cooked!" moaned the sugar glider. He threw his paws up in defeat.

"Bismark—" said Dawn.

But he would not let her speak. "I'll be minced

meat! Glider goulash! Marsupial mash!" Bismark placed a flap on his forehead, as though he were about to pass out. "I must keep watch. Sleep no more!" he continued, climbing to the top of a tree. "I shall be the eyes and ears for us all!"

The bats rolled their eyes. "He's on the edge, that chap."

"Completely *meshuggina*."

"The egg has cracked."

"Totally scrambled."

The others stayed quiet, but they were equally scared. The coyotes were not known for their kindness. In fact, they had a reputation for being scoundrels of the night.

Tobin surveyed the land, taking in the dim light as best as he could with his tiny eyes. Then he saw Dawn, who had wandered away, sitting alone on a grassy knoll. Slowly, the pangolin crawled toward his friend and sat down beside her.

Dawn let out a breath. She knew Tobin wanted an explanation.

"I have history with the coyotes," she started, her voice soft and low. "I met Ciro when I was young. We became good friends." She paused. "But we were born in remote northern brambles, away from other pups of our kind. We did not know the ways of the plains. And once we ventured out...well...." Dawn's words trailed off, and she lowered her gaze to the ground. "Ciro is a coyote. He belongs in a pack." Her voice hardened. "A pack of which I'm not a part."

Tobin waited, but the fox said no more. "Are you glad to see him?" he asked.

Dawn met Tobin's gaze. "We cannot deny our past," she explained. "Our memories define who we are."

Tobin did not know what exactly she meant, but he knew not to ask more. "I suppose this alliance is a good thing," he offered, hoping to show his support.

Dawn nodded. "It is certainly our best hope," she replied.

"Ayyyeeeeee!"

At the sound of the sugar glider's sharp wail, the fox's ears stood erect.

"Holy mother of madness! *El padre* of pain! It's the carnivores!" From his perch in the tree, Bismark jumped and pointed feverishly.

The animals turned in time to see three coyotes trotting toward them from the brush.

"*Au revoir, mis amigos*! I shall see you all in another life!" As Bismark lamented his fate, he lost his footing on a patch of slippery bark and tumbled out of the tree. With a grunt and a thump, the sugar glider landed on the moss beds below.

"Oh dear," said Tobin, stepping toward his fallen friend.

"He will be fine," said Dawn. She turned toward the coyotes. "Welcome, Ciro."

Ciro furrowed his brow, baffled by the odd assortment of creatures. Then he nodded to his companions.

"This is Ajax and Julian," he said. The giant creatures bowed in greeting. "Have the members of your group been caught up?"

"They have not," Dawn replied.

"Then that is where we'll begin." Ciro eyed Bismark, still lying in a heap. "Shall we wait for the flying squirrel?"

"Squirrel!" The bats howled with laughter.

"He's a marsupial, sir!"

"He'll tell you himself!"

"Soon as he wakes up from his fall!"

"Let's focus," said Dawn, shooting a stern look at the bats. The fox turned to Ciro. "Why don't you share what you know," she suggested. "We can fill Bismark in later."

"Very well," replied the coyote. He motioned for the group to draw closer. "We must stop these nocturnal nappings."

"We've been aware of them for some time," added Julian.

"Since one of our own was snatched!" Ajax barked. The vein in his neck pulsed with rage.

"Yes," Ciro said, "when our Audrey went missing." He took a deep breath. "Since then, we have confirmed the disappearance of many others. A raccoon, a possum, a wombat—"

Cora let out a small yelp.

Ciro paused for a moment then went on. "A honey badger, a mink, a tarantula…and twelve kiwis."

Julian bowed his head. Ajax clawed at the earth.

"We have been studying these animals," Ciro continued. "Their patterns, behaviors, and qualities. We need to know why they were taken."

The animals listened carefully. Even the bats were silent.

"But nothing adds up," finished Ciro. "There is no common thread among those who are missing." The coyote glanced over at Dawn. "We do, however, have one meaningful lead."

The others leaned in.

"There is one animal who's been spotted at every known napping." Ciro paused. "The jerboa."

Cora gasped. The bats flapped. But Tobin did not flinch.

"Yes," confirmed Dawn. She stepped beside the coyote. "Jerry's involvement is certain. He may be too small to overpower larger creatures, but he definitely played a role in their disappearance."

"Well, let's go find him then!" Ajax barked. The hot-tempered coyote scratched at the earth.

Ciro raised his front paw, signaling for his friend to calm down.

Ajax took a deep breath, but his eyes still gleamed with rage. "That rotten rodent is out there," he grunted, "just waiting to nap his next victim."

Tobin lowered his gaze toward the earth. "I never trusted him," he said softly.

"But Bismark did," said Dawn, "and Jerry trusted Bismark as well." Her lips curled up slightly.

"Is…is that a good thing?" asked Cora.

The fox nodded. "Jerry might have confided in him," she explained. "Let's go wake Bismark."

Ciro surveyed the nervous group. His face flashed with mischief. "Yes," he said. The coyote shot a sly wink at the bats "Let's go rouse the squirrel."

All four flying creatures tittered at Ciro's joke. Cora chuckled under her breath. Even Dawn flashed a grin. Despite the dangers that lurked, Tobin felt a wave of relief. The coyotes were friends, not foes. And together, they would restore safety and peace to the night.

Chapter Fifteen
THE ABDUCTION

"Stand back!" screeched Bismark, recoiling from Ciro in fear. "I can see the hunger in your eyes! There is very little meat on these bones, I'll have you know." Bismark awoke from his terrible fall to an actual nightmare—a coyote hovering inches above him.

"Bismark, stop." Dawn shook her head. "Ciro is not thinking about food right now. He just wants to know what Jerry told you."

"That's what he wants you to think, my sweet,

gullible fox. First he gets information, and then he begins preparation. What will it be this time, coyote? Sugar glider stew?" Bismark shuddered. "This is not how I want to go!" he exclaimed, flailing a fist through the air. "I intend to live forever, you know. Or at least I'll die trying!" Bismark raced up the tree trunk and hid in its limbs.

"Huh?" Ciro shook his head in confusion.

"He often makes little sense," whispered Cora.

The fox tilted her head toward the treetop. "Bismark, enough. Now tell us: what did the jerboa say?"

Bismark popped his head out from a tangle of leaves. "Nothing, *nada*, *rien*! He did not tell me anything." The sugar glider crawled to a far-reaching limb, where he plopped down on his behind.

The animals standing below slumped with discouragement. There was a moment of uneasy silence as they realized they had no more leads.

The sugar glider sighed and rubbed the back of his head. "Perhaps he went to find the last teammate," he said.

One by one, the other animals lifted their heads.

"What was that?" Dawn stood at the base of the tree, her eyes wide and alert.

"His *amigos*," Bismark continued. "They're almost together now. All but the final one." The sugar glider gazed into the distance, seemingly lost in thought.

The fox raised a paw to the bark, intrigued. "What '*amigos*'?" she asked.

"The group, the team, *la squadra*," he said, shifting his weight on the branch. "When he gathers them all, he can return to his family."

Ciro crept beside Dawn. "Bismark," he pressed, "what is this team?"

"Oh, you know." The sugar glider sighed. "The raccoon, the possum, the honey badger...."

"Is there a mink in this group?" Ciro asked.

"What about a coyote?" Ajax demanded.

"Ahhh...yes, I believe so." The sugar glider moved down a few branches.

Ciro and Dawn's eyes locked in a meaningful gaze. No one spoke.

"Now, Bismark," said Dawn. The fox spoke evenly, so as to not fluster her friend. "Did Jerry ever mention the purpose of this team?"

"Yes," chimed in Tobin. "What's it for?"

"No, no, no," said the sugar glider. "No mention of any of that. Though I did tell him that all teams need a great leader. A master of ceremonies. A *maestro*, like *moi*!" Bismark jumped to his feet and then bowed. "Yes, *maestro*. I rather like the ring of that."

Dawn and the others gasped. Had Bismark unknowingly volunteered to be napped?

The sugar glider stared at his friends. Then, suddenly, his eyes blazed with comprehension.

"*Mon dieu*!" he yelped. He cradled himself in his flaps and rocked back and forth. "What have I done?"

"Bismark, think," Dawn commanded. "What else did Jerry say?"

"Did he mention my brother?" cried Cora.

"Or Audrey?" boomed Ajax. "Did he ever mention the name Audrey?"

"Um...um...." Bismark wiped beads of sweat from his forehead.

"What's the nature of this team?" questioned Julian.

"Was he the leader?" asked Ciro.

"Oh *mon dieu*! *Mon dieu*!" Bismark paced on the branch, running his paws through his fur. "I...I...." He could no longer speak. The questions were coming too fast, and the little sugar glider could not handle the pressure. He was wheezing, his breath growing shallow. His eyes danced in their sockets. His body swayed. And then, with a crashing thud, he plummeted down from the tree. For the second time that night, the sugar glider lay on the ground, unconscious.

"*Klutz*!"

"Featherweight!"

"Squirrel!"

The bats giggled and snickered, but a shrill scream in the distance drowned out their jeers.

The coyotes bared their sharp fangs. Dawn arched her spine. Tobin and Cora huddled together.

"Another napping!" whispered the wombat.

"But where?" wondered Tobin.

The group turned their heads left and right, but they could not locate the source of the sound.

"Let's check the den!" Ajax roared. With an angry grunt, the coyote raced into the woods.

The rest of the animals followed, sprinting into the dark. But when they arrived at the den, it was empty. Panting and wheezing, the group scanned the land. There was no trace of the napper.

Dawn tilted her head toward the plains. "Maybe the sound came from that way," she said.

"Or that way," said Julian. The coyote pointed in the opposite direction.

The group stood in stupefied silence, unsure of what to do next.

Suddenly, the wombat let out a gasp. "Where's Tobin?"

Dawn's eyes darted left, then right. "No one panic," she said, though her own heart was racing. "Maybe he's with Bismark." The fox ran toward the tree where they'd left the unconscious glider. Sure enough, there stood Tobin.

"Your scales!" Cora cried.

Tobin's coat, normally smooth, was now scratched and scuffed all along his left side. The wombat lowered her gaze, pained at the sight of her injured friend.

But Tobin seemed unconcerned with his wounds. He was panting and flustered. "Oh goodness," he gasped, struggling to regain his breath. "They, they...."

Dawn met the pangolin's terrified gaze. "What is it?" she asked.

"They got him!" he sputtered. "They took Bismark!"

Chapter Sixteen
BIGGER BEASTS

"Awfully quiet."

"Rather miss the crazy rants."

"Just not quite right without the squirrel."

"*Svor.*"

The bats hung their heads low as they tended to Tobin's injured scales. As they slathered the wounds in a paste made from smashed cordyline leaves, Dawn pressed Tobin for more information.

"What do you remember?" she asked. Her tone

was gentle, yet urgent.

"Oh dear," said Tobin. "It was terrible!" The pangolin's breath was heavy, and his scales were still trembling with shock.

"Was it Jerry?" asked Julian.

Ajax arched his spine, and his wiry fur stood on end. "That scoundrel! I'm gonna...I'm gonna...." The coyote pawed the earth angrily.

Cora traced her paw over Tobin's injured scales. "But Jerry couldn't have hurt you this way. He's so small."

"Exactly," said Dawn. "The jerboa is far too small and too frail to inflict this sort of damage." The fox pointed to the claw pattern formed by the scratch marks on the pangolin's side. "These are the marks of a much bigger creature."

Tobin took a deep breath then exhaled. "Right," he said, growing calmer at last. "Jerry was not there at all."

The animals drew in closer, captivated by the pangolin's words.

"They were huge, like big lizards." Tobin's eyes flashed with fear. "They had long, knobby snouts.... And, oh goodness! They had terrible, gleaming white teeth."

"They?" Ajax asked. "There was more than one of these things?"

The pangolin nodded. "There were five."

"Sounds like crocs to me," said Julian.

"Crocodiles?" a few voices gasped. The bats shuddered under their wings. Cora covered her face with her paws.

"Jerry must be working with them," said the fox. "They must have recruited Bismark for this... team."

Ciro scratched his ear, searching his memory. "He did offer to be—what did he say?"

"The *maestro*," said Dawn. "The team leader."

Cora padded next to the fox. "I still don't understand," she began. "What's this team for?" Her voice quavered with deep concern.

"For crushing!"

"For chewing!"

"For chomping!"

The bats flapped their wings and spun round in circles.

"Chomping?" Cora yelped.

"*Svor*," said the bats. They all rubbed their bellies.

"Oh no!" Cora cried. Her eyes filled with tears. "My brother...Bismark...the kiwis...!"

"Stop that," snapped Dawn, glaring at the bats. "No one's been eaten."

Tobin laid a paw on Cora's back, hoping to comfort his furry friend. But he wondered how Dawn knew for certain.

"What makes you so sure?" asked Julian, voicing the pangolin's thoughts.

All eyes locked on Dawn. "It wouldn't make sense," she replied.

"Right," agreed Ciro. "Why would the crocs employ Jerry if they were just hunting for food? And why wouldn't they eat the jerboa? They can hunt perfectly well by themselves."

"We need to find them!" said Ajax. "We have no time to waste."

"But where are they?" asked Cora.

Dawn furrowed her brow. "It's strange," she began.

Everyone turned to face the fox.

"Crocodiles are saltwater creatures, yet they're forming a team way up here."

"Strange, indeed," added Tobin. "Everything seems out of place. Just like those sea cucumbers."

Dawn came to a halt. "That's it!" she said.

"What is?" asked Cora.

"I know how to find them," said Dawn. The fox gazed toward the river. "The crocs have been leaving a trail."

Tobin's eyes gleamed. He suddenly understood. "That's why the water was salty!" he said. "The crocodiles have been dragging up sea water."

"So...we follow the salt?" asked Cora.

"Exactly." Dawn stood and turned toward the group. "Follow me," she declared. "We are going back to the river."

Chapter Seventeen
THE LEGEND

Once again, Tobin felt out of breath. The group had raced to the river, back where they'd last seen the sea cucumbers. Desperate for a moment of rest, the pangolin slumped at the edge of an inlet. But then he noticed something strange. "Hmm," he murmured. "My eyes may be failing me, but look! There seems to be some sort of whirlpool."

The others drew close and crouched at the bank. Indeed, the water was swirling in circles.

"It looks like it's being sucked down," observed Dawn.

"Down where?" Cora asked.

Suddenly, Ciro sprung to his feet and locked eyes with the fox.

"Could it be?" whispered Dawn.

Ciro shook his head in disbelief. "I've heard of them only in legend."

Cora tilted her head, still confused. "Heard of what?"

The canines turned toward the group.

"Mystical underground caves," said Ciro. "It's said that rivers flow through them." He looked back at the mysterious whirlpool.

"But I didn't think they were real," added Dawn. Her voice sounded skeptical. "With their strange light? And rushing falls? It always sounded a little, well, made up."

The bats teetered forth.

"Strange light?" said a bat.

"Rushing falls?" said another.

"That stuff's real," said a third.

"Real as rabbit."

Ciro's eyes flashed with excitement. "What's that you say?" He moved toward the bats and crouched low. "You know of these caves?"

"*Svor.*"

"One right beneath us, in fact."

"Used to hang in there all the time."

"But it's crazy down there. Like a maze."

"*Svor.* You could get lost."

"Especially without sonar."

Dawn's ears stood tall and alert. "Can you take us there?" she requested. "The screams have all been in this area, and yet there are no traces of the missing animals." Dawn paused, seeming to piece together the information as she spoke. " No traces above ground that is, but I wonder what we might find if we go below."

"Into the caves then!" said one bat.

"To look for the traces."

"And the trouble!"

"Oh goodness," murmured Tobin, but he was nodding in agreement.

A rush of wind blew through the air, rustling the leaves on the trees. The leather-winged creatures stood still.

"Now," urged the fox. "Take us there now."

The bats glanced at each other, perplexed.

"But you're already here!" said one.

In unison, the foursome pointed at a hole in the

ground. It was about the width of a lemon.

"That's the entrance," finished another.

"Oh dear," Tobin muttered. He squinted at the tiny, dark entrance, and then eyed his own rounded belly. "That'll be a tight squeeze."

"There are more entrances," said a bat, "but next one's wayyyy down that way." He pointed downstream.

"Or, is it that way?" said another. This one pointed up.

The foursome stumbled back and forth, clearly confused.

"Julian, Ajax," said Ciro, "how long will it take you to widen this hole?"

The coyotes circled the opening, evaluating the composition and density of the dirt. The earth was packed and dry.

"Might take a while," said Julian.

"A while?" cried Cora. She shook her head and marched toward the hole. "We don't have 'a while'," she said. "Step aside."

The animals raised their brows at the normally docile wombat.

"Please," Cora added.

The coyotes stepped back as the wombat planted herself in front of the hole. She flexed her paws then dug her claws into the soil. Using all four limbs, she began to clear the debris, flinging rocks and dirt through the air. She even unearthed a few sticks that shot out behind her like spears.

Shielded by tree trunks and bushes, the animals watched the wombat burrow and plow. Then the shower of earth stopped. Slowly, the group emerged from their cover. As the air cleared, Cora beamed. Before her stood a gaping hole in the ground.

"Let's get down there," she said. "Now."

Chapter Eighteen
THE FACILITY

Creeping along single file, the animals descended into the earth.

"It's so dark," whispered Cora.

Tobin could not help but agree. The tunnel was narrow, and the damp walls were cold and rough. He followed behind the bats, who led the way through the winding underground maze.

After a series of tight corners, the cave suddenly expanded. The walls turned from dark dirt to glossy white stone that glowed with a strange blue light.

"I've never seen anything like this," said Dawn.

"Much too bright in this joint for us," said a bat, shielding his face with one wing.

"Couldn't sleep a wink down here," said another.

"It's beautiful," breathed Cora.

The animals continued on in silence, captivated by the ghostly light and long shadows. They began to lose sense of time. Was it still night? Was it morning? With no view of the sky, there was no way to tell.

Suddenly, Dawn drew to a halt.

"Shhh." She drew a paw to her lips. "I hear something."

Treading softly, the pack approached a bend in the path. The light grew brighter as they rounded the curve.

Cora gasped. Tobin gulped. Even the coyotes held their breath.

The cave opened up into a great, vaulted chamber with a huge marble floor. It was a flat, oblong surface that stretched from wall to wall and shone as though it were polished. Across its center was painted a vertical red line.

Waterfalls fed pools at both ends of the room. The churning water, which must have carved this natural cavern over thousands of years, glowed with sapphire light.

"The water's the source of the glow," whispered Ciro.

Dawn crept to the edge of the precipice and peered down. "Looks like Sea Sparkle," she said.

"Sea Sparkle?" Cora tilted her head. Her eyes flickered with blue.

"It's a tiny creature that lives in the ocean. It shimmers with the motion of the waves. I've seen it before, but only a few specks." The fox paused and turned back toward the glow. "Never so many. Never like this."

Ciro edged his way round the bats to stand next to Dawn. For a moment, they sat side-by-side and marveled at the beauty of the cave. But suddenly, a throaty bellow filled the room.

"Don't you dare argue with me," said the booming voice. "Do it now!"

Cora shuddered and nestled next to Tobin. Dawn's ears flicked on end.

"Y-y-yes. Yes, of course." A second voice floated through the air. "Okay th-then." This one was thin and nasal—and very familiar.

"Jerry!" whispered Tobin.

Ajax clawed the white marble ground. "Let's go!" he hissed. "I'll teach that jerboa not to lie to a coyote!"

Ciro placed a paw on his friend's back. "Hold on now," he said. "We can't afford to be careless."

"Yes, we need a plan," agreed Dawn. The fox looked over the room, taking in the height of the ceiling, the placement of the waterfalls. They were standing on an upper ledge that encircled the entire chamber. Closer to the ground was a tunnel leading deeper into the cave system. The voices sounded like they were echoing from below—that tunnel would be a good place to start looking.

Dawn turned toward the group. "Bats," she said, "you four keep watch. Remain undetected at all costs. That means no joking around."

"*Svor!*" They stood in line and saluted, their backs straight as sticks. Then, flapping their wings, they flew to the corners of the chamber. Gripping the stone with their feet, they dropped and hung upsidedown.

"Good," said Dawn. "The rest of us will go on."

"And find Jerry," said Tobin.

"Yes," agreed Dawn. "He holds the answers. It is time we go get them."

With a whoosh of her tail, the fox turned, and led the way down toward the glowing floor of the cave.

Chapter Nineteen
FEATHERS AND FUR

"Um... You g-guys? Coach says he needs you b-b-back out there."

Dawn raised a paw to call for silence. Jerry's voice echoed out from a passageway that connected to the main floor of the cave. The fox led the animals down the passage to the opening of a dark chamber. A large boulder sat outside the entrance, providing a good place to hide and listen to the conversation inside.

"I'm s-s-sorry," said the jerboa. "But those are d-d-direct orders."

A chorus of groans filled the air.

"Already?"

"Impossible!"

"We just finished our last set of drills!"

Tobin sniffed the air. "I smell them," he whispered. "Sweat, fear—oh goodness, I hope they're all right!"

Dawn craned her neck to peek around the rock. But she quickly drew back at the sound of a thunderous voice:

"JERRY!" it boomed.

"Y-y-y-yes, Coach?"

Heavy, menacing steps echoed down the passageway. The animals scrambled to the far side of the boulder, hiding themselves from view. Ciro moved to look at the source of the footsteps, but Dawn stopped him with a shake of her head. They could not risk being seen. The steps thundered into the room.

"Oh, hel-l-lo," Jerry stammered. "We were just c-c-coming out."

There were a few muffled groans.

"Actually," ventured a voice, "we were wondering: could we take the day off?"

A giant roar filled the air. "There will be no days off! Not till I face those other coachers. Now back on the floor!"

122

There was a shuffling of paws as the weary animals obeyed. Then silence.

The fox pricked her ears. "They're gone," she announced. She motioned everyone forward. "Let's go investigate while we can."

"Ajax, Julian," Ciro said, "you stay here. We might need some assistance if something goes wrong."

The two coyotes melted into the shadows while the rest of the group crept into the recently vacated room. It was roughly square, with a low uneven ceiling. The floor was covered in debris. What little light there was came from a small trickle of glowing water that ran down from a crack in the wall.

"Remember, keep quiet," said the fox.

Lowering his nose to the ground, Tobin sniffed for clues. "I think I smell...yes!" The pangolin held up a smooth strand of fur. "A mink!"

"And look," Ciro said. The coyote pawed at a clump of bristly brown feathers.

"Feathers and fur," said the wombat. She cocked her head to the side. "What does this mean?"

"It means we found them," said Dawn. "The missing nocturnals are here."

Cora's eyes flashed with hope.

"And Bismark might be right," said Tobin. "It sounds as if they're on some sort of team."

"Wait!" cried the wombat. "What's this?"

The other three gathered round. In Cora's paw was a brown, jagged sliver of some hard material.

"Keratin," Tobin said. "Like my scales."

Dawn examined the remnant. "It's from a bird's beak," she whispered.

Tobin and Cora both gulped.

Dawn's auburn fur rose on end. "I found something else." Slowly, she bent toward a small, off-white object. "A tooth."

Cora let out a yelp. "It's a wombat's tooth!"

"Quiet!" said Ciro. He drew his paw to his lips. Someone was coming.

"Y-y-yes, Coach! As you wish!" Jerry's distinct, timid voice bounced off the stone walls. The jerboa entered the room. "I'll b-b-be right back, just one—" At the sight of the familiar creatures, he froze. Then he spun toward the entrance to flee.

But Ciro was already blocking the way. Jerry was trapped.

Chapter Twenty
NEW RECRUITS

"D-d-don't eat me," pleaded Jerry in a whisper. His large ears flopped over his face. "I didn't d-do anything wrong!"

"We don't have much time," said the fox. She towered over the tiny jerboa. "Tell us what you know. Where are they?"

"They're all here! You've got to believe me! I had no ch-choice!"

"Jerry," said Dawn, "I don't want to lose my temper."

But the jerboa kept on. "I s-swear, I'm b-b-barely involved! The jerboas just sweep the floor during breaks with our tails." We don't even play!"

"Play what, exactly?" asked Dawn.

"The game," Jerry said. "Y-you know, with the team."

"What sort of game?" Ciro asked. His voice was tinged with impatience. "Stop talking in circles."

Glancing over his shoulder, Jerry eyed the coyote and gulped. "Oh, well, it's h-h-hard to explain...."

Dawn extended her claws and took a slow step toward the jerboa.

"R-r-right," Jerry stammered. "The game. It's the one with the sticks. I mean, birds! Beaks! You know, you hit the spider and try to score."

The animals exchanged confused looks. They had never heard of such a game.

"Whose idea is this?" Ciro asked.

"Yes," pressed the fox. "Who is this 'Coach' you were talking to?"

Suddenly, the jerboa's ears stood on end.

Boom, boom, boom.

Heavy footsteps.

"Oh d-d-dear." Jerry crouched into a ball. "It's him!"

Dawn searched the room for a place to hide, but it was too late.

"Well, well, well." A deep baritone voice thrummed from the shadows. "What do we have here?"

Suddenly, the footsteps multiplied.

Boom. Boom. Boom. Boom. Boom. Boom.

"Oh goodness!" Tobin gasped.

A giant crocodile thundered into the room. His body, at least ten feet long, was covered in mud-colored scales. Two rows of jagged spikes ran down his back. He was flanked by five smaller crocs.

"C-Coach Boris!" said the jerboa. "Please, d-d-don't hurt my family! I don't know how these intruders got in here!"

Ignoring Jerry, Boris eyed the newcomers. Then he leaned back his head and cackled, exposing his long curved teeth. His five followers did the same.

"Oh, little Jerry." The croc thumped his long tail on the ground. "No need to fret. You've done nothing wrong."

Jerry gazed up at the reptile. "I... I haven't?"

"On the contrary," said Boris, "I'm quite pleased."

"You... y-you are?"

Boris walked up to Tobin, sticking his pointed

127

snout in the pangolin's face.

"A natural armor. Most interesting." He ran a claw down the side of Tobin's shuddering scales. "Might be useful on defense."

He turned his head to Cora. She was clenching her paws, trying her best not to quiver noticeably.

"Another wombat, huh? I hope you're better than the other one I have. He's worthless."

Ciro was the next in line. He peeled back his lips and snarled as the crocodile approached. Boris leaned his head back for a short, sharp laugh.

"Ha! You can always trust a coyote to bring that scrappy fighting spirit! I can tell you will do quite well here."

Finally, the croc made his way over to Dawn.

"Now, this is promising. A fox! And an excellent specimen, at that: strong, slender, and sturdy. Perhaps the perfect build for an offensive player!"

As Boris looked her over, Dawn could tell that he was clutching something in his fist.

"I am pleased, indeed," said Boris. He glanced at the trembling jerboa. "You've done well, little one. This is a delightful surprise." The croc tossed the object he held up in the air. Then he caught it absent-mindedly. It was a small red cylinder with a shiny, coppery glow at one end. His eyes blazed with excitement. "Miss, Bee, Hay, Vee, Orr!" Boris's five henchmen stood at attention. "Bring our new friends to the prison chamber."

The swarm of crocs crowded in on the animals. Before they knew it, Cora, Ciro, Dawn, and Tobin were pinned to the floor.

Ciro snarled and tried to bite the two crocs who held him.

"There, there," Boris said. He scoffed at the squirming coyote. "It's a rough game, so you better get used to a few bumps and bruises."

Miss, Bee, Hay, Vee, and Orr laughed in agreement. Boris flipped the strange cylinder up in the air again.

"Now, I wish I could welcome you properly, but I have a practice to lead." With a sharp whip of his tail, the croc turned away. "I will deal with my new recruits later."

Chapter Twenty-One
TRAPPED

"Come on," Ciro urged. Once again, the coyote hurled his weight into the stone. The crocs had blocked the entrance to their new prison with a heavy boulder, completely sealing the prisoners in. The coyote could not get the stone to budge.

"Oh goodness," Tobin said. He and Cora rested against the far wall. "Be careful!"

Ciro shook out his shoulder. "Just a few more tries," he insisted. "I'll get us out."

Dawn shook her head. "You haven't changed a bit."

At this, Ciro turned. "What's that?"

"Brute force won't fix everything," Dawn continued. "You're acting the way you did as a pup. Always chewing through coconuts when you could just drop them on rocks."

Ciro grinned. "I still do that, you know."

Despite her best efforts, Dawn could not keep from smiling.

Ciro drew close to the fox. "I still think about you," he admitted.

A softness fell on Dawn's face, and she let her eyes lock on Ciro's. Then she lowered her gaze. "But I'm still a *vulpes*, and you a *canis*," she sighed. "I will never be part of your pack."

Ciro opened his mouth to respond, but a loud, sing-songy voice rang out first.

"Me-me-me-meeeeeeee!"

Tobin and Cora scurried over and pressed their ear against the stone.

"What was that?" Cora asked.

"La-la-la-laaaaaaaaa!" The voice sang out again.

"So strange," Ciro muttered.

"Yet so familiar," said Dawn. The fox moved

toward the boulder. Then she crouched to inspect a crack where it met the wall. A soft glow shone from the other side. Tilting her head, she peered through. "Bismark!" she called.

The singing came to a halt.

"Dawn?" said the voice. "Is that you? Or are the walls so moved by the sound of my singing that they call my name?"

The fox rolled her eyes. "Yes," she replied. "It's me. We're behind the boulder."

There was the scurrying of steps as the sugar glider rushed toward his love. "My sweet!" he exclaimed. Desperately, he flung himself at the stone and wormed his head through the crack. It was a little too narrow for him to squeeze all the way through. "I knew we'd meet again, *ma chèrie*! True love always prevails."

"Bismark," whispered Dawn, "listen carefully. Ciro's two friends, Ajax and Julian, are standing guard nearby. You need to find them and bring them here." The fox moved in closer. "Do you understand?"

"Yes, whatever you ask! I will bring you the moon, the stars, the heavens themselves!" He closed his eyes. Visions of Dawn danced in his head, her face awash with Sea Sparkle light.

"With the coyotes' help," she continued, "we can

move this boulder aside."

Bismark's eyes burst open. "Coyotes? Excuse me? *Pardon*?"

"The coyotes are not to be feared," Dawn said.

"It's true!" said Tobin. "They've been friendly and loyal."

Ciro smiled and placed his paw over Dawn's. "We work well together," he said.

Bismark glared at the two touching paws. His bald patch turned a deep red. "No! *Absolutamente* no!" he cried out. "This is an outrage! I will not cooperate with these canines!"

"You better keep your voice down," cautioned Ciro.

"Hush, mush!" said the sugar glider. "Do you know who you're talking to?"

Ciro scratched his head in confusion. "Your name is Bismark, right?"

"I may be small in stature but I am important! I'm the announcer, the songster, the *maestro*! I am an esteemed member of the Nocturnal Brigade! I am—"

Boom. Boom.

"—busted."

Bismark froze.

"What do we have here?"

The sugar glider popped his head out of the crack in the rock. Then, slowly, he spun around to face the fiery-eyed Boris.

"Welcoming the captives, I see," said the croc.

"No, no, no! In fact, I was just telling them how repulsivo they are!" Bismark forced a charming little grin.

But the giant reptile was not fooled. "Crocs!"

At once, Miss, Bee, Hay, Vee, and Orr came thumping to their leader's side.

"Yes, Boss?" said Bee.

"What's the trouble?" asked Vee.

Boris crossed his arms and glared at the sugar glider. "The *maestro* is the trouble. Lock this traitor squirrel up here with the others." The crocodile's long mouth curved ever so slightly into a smile. "I'd like a moment to consider my options."

Chapter Twenty-Two
THE JERBOA'S TALE

"Nonsense!" exclaimed Bismark. "That swamp-dwelling reptile will come to his senses in no time. I am his most valuable asset! You can't treat your talent this way!"

The animals groaned. With Bismark now trapped in the chambers too, there was no one to fetch Ajax and Julian. They were stuck, just like before.

"You can't fit through that crack?" asked Ciro.

"*Absolument pas!*" said the sugar glider. He

placed his hands on his hips. "How many times must I say it? I'm not some pygmy flying squirrel! I'm larger than I look, you know."

The coyote sighed.

"Maybe Ajax and Julian will find us," said Tobin. "We shouldn't give up hope just yet, right?"

"Doubtful," said the sugar glider. "These caves are crazy, I tell you. Mazes! Labyrinths! Impossible to navigate…without prior experience, that is."

"What can we do now? We're trapped here forever!" Cora sobbed.

The fox furrowed her brow. She had a plan. "Well, Bismark can still prove of use."

With a flourish of his cape, the sugar glider bowed. "But of course I can, foxy dame! I am the most useful of the useful. Name anything! Anything at all. A soothing song? A sweet caress? What do you desire, my lady?"

"What I desire is information." She stepped toward Bismark. "Tell us about this game."

"Ah, yes, the game," said the sugar glider. "Well, you see, it's all about balance. A delicate combination of pitch, tenor, and strength."

Tobin cocked his head. "Pitch?" he asked. "You mean…throwing?"

"No, no, no, my scaly *amigo*. Pitch! As in key! Notes! Song! I am speaking of my role as announcer!"

Dawn took a deep breath. "Bismark, we need to know about the actual game. What happens on the floor out there?"

Bismark let out a disinterested sigh. "As you wish, *mon amour*. Though I shall keep my explanation brief." He raised a paw to this throat. "Can't tax the vocal cords."

Ciro growled with impatience.

"Okay, okay!" Bismark shielded himself with his flaps. "It's quite simple, really. There are six players on each team. Using the kiwis, they slide the tarantula across the floor. I think his name is Harry—poor fellow, always getting bruised up, but that's the game. To win, you must hit the spider into the goal more times than the other team. So far, it has been the kidnapped animals against the crocs, but the crocs have completely outplayed them. The mink, raccoon, and coyote are on offense. The honey badger and possum play defense. Wombat's in goal."

"Wombat!" cried Cora. "Is it Joe? Is it my brother?"

Bismark scratched at his bald spot. "*Oui*? Yes? I think so? You both have that peculiar habit of shaking and quivering in difficult moments."

Cora sighed with relief. "That's Joe."

The fox shook her head from side to side. "Poor animals," she muttered, "being used like this for sport."

"And the jerboas?" pressed Ciro.

"What about the jerboas?" A voice echoed from behind the boulder.

The animals froze.

"Who's there?" Ciro called.

There was the scurry of tiny feet. Two big, floppy ears poked their way through the crack.

"Jerry?" Tobin asked.

"What do you want?" growled Ciro. "You've caused enough trouble here." He stepped alongside Tobin.

Jerry wedged the rest of his body through the tiny opening then dusted himself off. "Please," he began, "just let me explain."

Ciro snarled and bared his sharp teeth, but Dawn raised her paw.

Jerry gulped. "I know I've caused much disruption. Much pain. But I've acted out of pure desperation." The jerboa lowered his eyes to the floor. "Boris has all of us. Almost every jerboa there is. Unless I do what he asks, he'll kill us all!"

"I don't understand," said Tobin. "What is he making you do?"

Jerry clasped his paws at his chest. "Boris is clumsy and large," he began. "He never could've pulled this off alone. He needed an accomplice. Someone small, stealthy, and swift. Someone who could locate the players in secret."

"So it was you," said the coyote. "You led the crocs to the valley. You knowingly put others at risk."

"Yes! Yes!" Jerry cried. "I led the crocs to their victims, and watched as they dragged them into the river! I found them all! The kiwis, the mink, the coyote, the tarantula, the possum, the honey badger!" He glanced toward Cora. "And the wombat!"

Tobin took Cora's paw in his own.

"And *moi*!" cried Bismark.

"Yes," Jerry blubbered, "you too. I knew it was wrong, but I didn't know what else to do. One day, the crocs trapped us all inside our burrow. Then they marched us down here into these caves. Boris threatened to kill them if I didn't help him. My species is already endangered. If Boris killed them, we'd have no hope." The jerboa gulped. "We'd go extinct!"

"Oh goodness," uttered Tobin. He shivered at the sound of that word, so final, so harsh.

141

The room was quiet.

"But I know this is not an excuse," Jerry said. His voice was trembling as he wiped tears from his cheeks. "I have betrayed my fellow nocturnals. I'm a traitor of the night!" Jerry broke down in sobs.

Ciro circled the room then stood before the jerboa. "I am sorry for your species' fate," he declared, "but these are serious crimes you've committed."

The jerboa sniffed and wiped his cheeks dry. "I know," he agreed. He raised his large eyes. "That's why I've come to help."

"You…you're here to help?" Tobin asked.

Jerry nodded.

Ciro eyed the jerboa. "Haven't we learned not to trust him at this point?"

Dawn straightened her spine. "He's our only hope of escape," she replied. "Plus, he can never prove himself worthy if he is not given the chance."

Ciro cast his eyes down at the floor. "I suppose we don't have much to lose."

"Jerry," said Dawn, "you can fit through that space, correct?"

The jerboa smiled. "With room to spare," he said.

"All right," said the fox. "Huddle in, everyone."

The pack of animals whispered and plotted.

"That should work," Ciro said.

"Yes," agreed Jerry. "I'll be back right away!" The jerboa spun toward the exit.

"Jerry!" called Tobin. "Before you go, I must say… I've noticed you're barely stammering."

Jerry bowed his head, trying to hide the sheepish grin lifting his whiskers. "That's 'cause I'm telling the truth!" Then, with a flick of his tail, he ducked through the hole and ran off into the caves.

Chapter Twenty-Three
THE CHALLENGE

"I'm back!" called the jerboa. He slipped through the crack in the boulder, holding one end of a long, sturdy vine.

"Did you find Julian and Ajax?" asked Dawn.

"They're right outside. Boy, those two were not happy to see me! They chased me in circles for five minutes before I convinced them I wasn't playing any tricks."

Ciro shrugged as he took hold of the vine. "I don't blame them."

"Go and give the coyotes the signal," Dawn said. The jerboa saluted and wormed his way back through the rock.

The others quickly fell into position. Ciro stood facing the boulder. Then Dawn lifted Tobin and placed him atop Ciro's head. The clumsy pangolin lurched and wobbled as Ciro reared up on his hind legs.

"Oh goodness!" cried Tobin. He was about to fall, and the coyote was losing his balance trying to keep Tobin upright. Bismark rushed over and leaned into Ciro's leg to lend some stability.

"You can do it, *mes amis*! We will escape this cursed dungeon!"

Dawn looked on in disbelief. Was Bismark really helping Ciro?

The sugar glider glanced at Dawn, as if he had heard her thoughts. "I do what I must for the good of us all," Bismark said. He cleared his throat awkwardly.

Wasting no time, Dawn leapt onto Ciro's back and then climbed up onto Tobin's scales. Finally, Bismark glided over and stood on the fox's head.

"Now the vine," said Dawn.

Carefully, the animals passed up the vine. The

stack of creatures was just tall enough to reach the seam where the boulder met the opening in the wall. Up here, like down below, was a thin crack. Dawn fed the vine to Bismark, and then Bismark fed it through the narrow opening.

"Do you see it?" called Dawn to the coyotes outside.

"Got it!" said Ajax.

"Good," said the fox. "One more time."

The animals repeated the process on the other side, forming a loop around the boulder. Out in the cave, Ajax and Julian each took one end of the vine in their jaws. They pulled together, muscular necks bulging, until the huge stone nudged to the side.

"Success!" said the sugar glider. He sidled next to the fox. "It has been too long since we have worked together like this, you know."

Dawn raised a paw to call for silence. "Now remember," she whispered, "let's all keep quiet. The echoes will give us away if we're not careful."

The animals nodded. With Dawn in the lead, they crept down the hall.

"Yes," roared a voice. "Unexpected indeed!"

The group froze.

"It's the coach!" whispered the sugar glider.

"Those are Boris's private quarters," said Jerry. He pointed toward a small chamber farther down the passageway.

Dawn tiptoed forward and peered around the edge of the wall. All six crocodiles stood inside. From her position, she could see and hear everything—a perfect opportunity for a little eavesdropping. The other animals had crouched behind her and were listening as well.

"We'll hold a scrimmage," said Boris. "That's it! We'll have the old recruits play the new." He paced back and forth. "At the end, I will choose the top six to play in the big game."

"Yeah," said Bee.

"Top six," said Orr.

The crocodiles rubbed their claws together.

"Uh, coach?" asked Hay. "What big game?"

Boris roared and stomped toward the croc. "You haven't been paying attention! The big game! The one we've been working for!" Boris snorted then spat on the floor. "Those coachers will come back to play," he continued. "They'll be here once I've got a good team." The crocodile unclenched his fist. He was still holding that small, red tube in his palm.

Curious, the fox squinted. As Boris stared down

at the object, she thought his eyes looked almost sad. Dawn wondered what this red tube could be—and what it meant to the fearsome crocodile.

Suddenly, the crocodile shut his fist and punched it high in the air. "I will challenge these coachers!" he yelled. "I will show them a real, skilled, trained team. Then, finally, everything we lost will be returned!"

His five followers snapped their jaws with excitement. Boris pounded the floor with his tail.

"What's a coacher?" whispered Tobin.

Jerry shrugged. "He calls himself that, but I think he means 'Coach.' I'm not about to correct him anytime soon."

Dawn motioned for silence.

"Now, I think it's time to evaluate our new captives." The crocodile flashed his sharp teeth. "We'll see if they're of more use as players...or provisions."

The reptiles erupted in laughter.

Having heard enough, Dawn stepped forward into the room. The others followed close behind. "No," she declared. "You will not."

Chapter Twenty-Four
THE WAGER

"How did you all get out?" cried the crocodile. "That stone takes two crocodiles to move!"

"It's time we talked, Boris. There is no—"

Boris lunged forward, jaws wide open, roaring at the top of his lungs. Dawn felt his hot, damp breath on her face. He swung at her with his tail, but she dodged the blow. The crocodile followed up his first attack with a swipe of his claws. This time, he connected. He

151

scooped up the fox and flung her across the room toward his followers.

"No one disobeys me! I am the coacher!" shouted Boris. "I am the coacher!" The croc spun to face his cronies. "Why don't you show our prisoners back to their cell? And take this fox to my dining quarters. She'll be a great midnight snack." Boris's tongue traced the jagged outline of his teeth.

Miss, Bee, Hay, Vee, and Orr scrambled into action, surrounding the fox and her companions from all sides.

"Wait!" Dawn cried. The crocodiles were closing in on them. "I have a suggestion. A suggestion that you'll want to hear."

Tobin gulped. Dawn's voice, always steady and calm, was trembling.

"A suggestion? Do you really think you're in a position to suggest anything right now?" Boris snickered, and cleaned bright red fox hairs from the underside of his long claws.

"It has to do with your game."

Boris narrowed his eyes. "If you would have your last words be a suggestion, then so be it. What do you have in mind?"

"Well, you've been training this team now for a

while." The cunning fox stared straight at Boris. "This game must be very important. Are you sure you're ready?"

Boris eyed the red tube in his hand. Then he clenched his large fists.

"Of course we're ready!" he raged. "I am a coacher now! And I will take my team to meet the other coachers. They will be there. They must! It is time for their return." The croc paused, as if lost in a memory. "I've been preparing for this all year," he said, "gathering the best of the best."

Dawn furrowed her brow. Who were these other "coachers"? And what was a "coacher," exactly? Though she could not help but wonder, these questions would have to wait. There were other matters to address at the moment. She had found her angle.

"You say you have the best of the best, Boris," she said. "I have a proposition for you. A bet." The fearless fox drew even closer to the crocodile.

Miss, Bee, Hay, Vee, and Orr stared in awe. No one dared challenge their leader.

"We will play you," she said. She gestured at Tobin, Cora, and the coyotes. "We will play you and your crocs."

There was a moment of silence. Then Boris threw

his head back with laughter. "Silly fox!" he exclaimed.

His fellow crocodiles joined in the mockery, slapping their knees and clutching their sides.

"You had me there for a second," said Boris, "but you haven't even played the game once! You won't be able to balance on the marble, let alone swing your kiwi! Besides, it requires a deep level of strategy—you'll never be able to beat us on your first try!"

"All the more reason to take the bet." Dawn's tail twitched.

"You might have a point." The croc glanced at the small, red tube in his claws. Then he snapped back to attention. "What are your terms, fox?"

Miss, Bee, Hay, Vee, and Orr exchanged confused looks. Was Boris actually considering this bet?

"Your captives must be worn out by now," said Dawn. "And I hear they haven't been playing up to their potential. They're no match for you and your crocs."

Boris stared at the ground. It was true. The honey badger had a bum knee, the mink had sprained her ankle, and the possum was nearly blind. Plus, the wombat would not stop complaining about his missing tooth.

"We crocodiles won't be the ones playing the coachers," he grunted, "if that's what you're getting at."

"That's not what I'm suggesting. If you beat us, you can handpick your players from both your team and ours. You'll have the six best of twelve. But if we win," Dawn said, "then you must set us free. All of us."

"I was going to take the six best anyway!" The crocodile leaned his head back and laughed. "Why do I need to accept your bet at all?"

"Because without something to play for, we have no motivation to try. And if you don't see us play our absolute hardest, how will you know who is the best? This is the only way to judge our true potential. It's a safe bet for you—if you think your crocs can beat us."

"There is no doubt about it—you will lose." Boris scratched a patch of itchy scales under his chin as he studied Dawn nose to tail. "I do need the very best players, and I would rather not spend any more time arguing about this." The croc paced the room and tossed the red tube up in the air over and over again.

Finally, he turned to face Dawn.

"You have a deal. But with one more condition." Boris leaned in close and exhaled. His hot breath blew Dawn's fur back. "When I win," said the croc, "I keep the six best to play—"

"Yes," said the fox.

"And I keep the rest, too," said the croc. "To

do with as I please." Boris flashed a wicked grin, baring his rows of sharp fangs. A thick strand of saliva dangled from his lip. "That's the best offer you'll get."

Dawn stared at Boris. Her heart jumped in her chest. There was no backing out at this point. "We have a deal," said the fox.

They shook paws, and Boris marched toward the door. A sly smirk cracked his lips as he rounded the corner. The fox had played right into his hands.

Chapter Twenty-Five
THE FIRST VICTORY

"Ladies aaannnd gentlemen," announced Bismark from his perch above the center line, "take a look at that fox!"

All eyes were on Dawn as she warmed up on the marble. Ciro was good. Cora was decent. The others struggled to stay on their feet, let alone control the tarantula. But Dawn maneuvered her kiwi with skill and slid on the marble surface with grace. The fox was a natural.

"She must be shut down!" Boris whispered. His team gathered around him at the far goal. "Shut down, do you hear me? Bee, do not leave her uncovered for a moment. Hay, you mind the sweep, and Miss, don't forget to fall back on defense every play. If they get a fast break, let me stop it alone. I can handle anything they throw at me. Am I understood?"

"Yes, Coach," they said.

"We can't take any chances with that one." Boris watched as the fox spun in tight circles, with Harry balanced on the tip of her kiwi. "She is the threat."

"What a match we have here today!" Bismark exclaimed. "Finesse versus power, captor versus captive, the Nocs versus the Crocs! Are you ready for this, ladies and gentlemen?" Bismark looked down at the crowd of several hundred jerboas and the other captured nocturnals. "Hello? *Hola*?" he prompted. But there was no reply. The animals sat blankly on the stone benches encircling the floor. They were not in the mood to be entertained.

Boris slid over to where Dawn and her team were practicing. "Are you all ready to play?"

"We could use a little more time to get used to this surface," said Dawn.

"You've had enough time!" roared the croc.

158

"Besides, there's only one way to learn, and that's to play. We start in three minutes. Bats! Bismark! You hear that?"

The bats flapped down to the floor. With white marble dust, they had painted vertical stripes on their fur.

Bismark eyed their design. "Do not be fooled by the cheap imitation, folks! Those are refereeing bats, not sugar gliders! I assure you that the stripe down my back is *au naturel*."

Dawn moved toward the croc. "Before we start," she said, "we have one last condition."

Boris spun and stuck his snaggletoothed snout in Dawn's face. "No more conditions. We play for freedom, your team versus mine. The agreement has been struck!"

Dawn did not budge. She stared into the crocodile's yellow eyes. "Yes," she said, her voice calm. "We play for freedom. But you must honor that freedom with an act of faith. A sign of your good word."

Boris let out a long, hissing breath through his nostrils. "And what is this act of faith—this proof of my good word?"

Dawn raised her chin. "You must release the jerboas. Only when they are free will we play this game." The fox looked out at the tiny animals clustered around the floor. They were squeaking and whispering in disbelief.

"Impossible!" Boris bellowed, silencing the crowd. "I will release no one! No one! I mean, unless, of course, you win. Besides, the jerboas are necessary to maintain the marble rink. Impossible to play without them."

"Actually, we have brought lomandra leaves from above ground," Dawn replied. "We will fashion the leaves into brooms that will keep the marble clean— better than the jerboas' tails ever could."

The crocodile and the fox locked eyes. Finally, the croc flinched.

"Fine!" Boris grunted. "The jerboas may go. They are of no use to me anyway." The crocodile dismissed the rodents with a petulant wave of his claw.

The jerboas erupted in cheering and song as they hugged and danced at the news of their release.

"Thank you, thank you, thank you!" they cried. In a flood, they made their way toward the exits. Only Jerry remained quiet.

"Wait!" he called over the crowd. "Brothers, sisters, my jerboa kin!"

The jerboas quieted. All eyes in the arena fell on the tiny desert rodent.

160

Jerry drew in a deep breath, steeled his nerves, and spoke. "We will stay."

A silence fell on the cave.

"I made the mistake of helping to bring our nocturnal brethren here, but we cannot make the mistake of leaving them now. We must stay to the finish. Whatever the finish may be." With that, Jerry turned and slowly walked to the sidelines where he seated himself on a bench.

For a few moments, none of the jerboas moved. But then, one by one, they returned to their seats. Hundreds of them, row after row, lined up on the cold, hard, stone benches.

"Let's go, Nocs!" shouted Jerry, breaking the silence. The crowd erupted in cheers.

Boris's eyes blazed with fury. "Enough interruptions!" he roared, desperate to regain control. "It's time to face off."

Chapter Twenty-Six
NOCS VERSUS CROCS

"*Un, deux, trois*...game on!"

At Bismark's call, the bats dropped Harry onto the floor. The second he hit the ground, the tarantula curled into a tight ball, tucking in his legs as tight as he could.

Dawn and Miss swiped their kiwis. Pushing Dawn to the side, the crocodile tucked the tarantula into the crook of her kiwi's beak. Miss glided on the slick floor, maneuvering around the challengers who were swiping at the spider. Past Ciro, slap, slap, she whacked Harry back and forth, slap, slap, past Ajax and Julian, slap, slap, she slid over to the side of the rink, pulling an inexperienced Cora and Tobin away from the goal. The Nocs raced after them, but their balance was shaky on the strange, slippery surface, and they had limited control of their kiwis. Miss slid a pass to Vee, standing behind Tobin and Cora, who tapped the tarantula into the open net.

On the next possession, Orr received the first pass. He cocked his kiwi back and gave Harry a whack, sending the spider whistling into the goal. The Crocs were up two points to zero, and the first period wasn't even halfway over.

"Oh goodness!" The pangolin paced in front of the goal. "It's all a blur! I should never have agreed to be the goalie. My vision's too weak for this game!"

Cora placed a paw on Tobin's back.

"You can do this," she said. "You don't have to rely on your sight."

The pangolin rubbed his eyes. "What do you mean?"

Cora smiled. "Look at the bats," she said. "They can't see at all! They just use their ears."

Tobin glanced at his leather-winged friends.

164

Although they were stumbling a bit, they did seem to know where they were.

"You know what a tarantula smells like, right?" Cora asked.

Tobin's face brightened. He nodded and tapped his nose twice. He was ready.

"Face-off!" yelled the sugar glider.

The tarantula was dropped once again. After the face-off, Miss and Bee took control of Harry and zoomed past Ajax and Dawn. Ciro swiped the spider away for a moment, but lost possession on an unlucky bounce. The Crocs regained control and were soon bearing down on the goal.

"Prey on the pangolin!" hissed Bee.

Miss cackled and increased her speed.

"Oh goodness," Tobin murmured. The on-slaught of reptiles was once again headed his way.

Cora looked up at her brother in the stands. Joe was quivering, his paws over his eyes, unable to watch the blowout. His lips were curled up, revealing the dark gap where his missing tooth used to be. The wombat clenched her jaw and tightened her paws around her kiwi. No one was going to score on her goal again. Without a second thought, she shot like a bolt down the marble toward the two advancing players.

"No you don't!" Cora hollered, leaping into the air with every drop of strength in her legs. The crocodiles raised their kiwis to start their backswing, but Cora was there to block the shot. She came down hard on her bottom, right on top of the furry spider. Splat!

"WZZZZ!" The bats whistled through their crooked teeth, waving their wings madly.

Harry's eight limbs splayed out in every direction underneath the wombat's behind. His fangs were stuck like ice picks into the marble slab.

"Ohhhh," Harry groaned. His eight eyes were crossed and spinning in their sockets. "I got biffed by a buttock!"

"Oh! Oh, I'm sorry!" Cora repeated her apologies over and over as she lifted herself up off of Harry. "I don't know what came over me."

"Ladies and gentlemen!" said Bismark. "Roughing the spider!"

Boris clapped his claws and cheered at the top of his lungs. "Wonderful! Wonderful!" he screamed. "A power play for the Crocs! See you later, wombat!"

Shocked, Cora glanced at the fox. But Dawn confirmed the call with a shrug. By the rules of the game, the wombat was forced to sit out for the rest of the period, leaving the Nocs one player short.

Cora slumped toward the sidelines, her gaze glued to the floor. She had tried to be great and heroic, but she had only been clumsy and harmful. "He'll be so disappointed," she muttered, looking back at her brother. But when Cora met Joe's gaze, his eyes were full of pride.

"WZZZZ!" The bats whistled to restart the game. With a sigh, Harry curled back into a ball and squeezed his eyes shut.

Clack! With a powerful strike, Miss got a hold of the spider.

"Please be gentle!" begged the kiwi. "My beak is terribly scratched from this hard floor!"

"Quiet!" snapped Miss. With Vee right beside her, the croc moved skillfully around the defense. In an attempt to use up the time, she played the spider back to her own goal. Then, in the period's final moments, Vee slapped a shot straight through Tobin's legs.

The bats whistled to send both teams to the bench for intermission. The score was three to zero in favor of the Crocs, and there were still two more periods left to play.

"*Qué lástima*! We have a tragic night in the making here, ladies and gentlemen," groaned Bismark. "Can our beloved Nocs pull themselves together, or will we be spending the rest of our nights in this cave? I, for one, have not lost hope yet!"

Boris clapped as his team gathered round. "Wonderful! Now that's how you move the tarantula!" With a big, toothy grin, he congratulated each of his players. Then he turned toward the sideline. "Jerry!" he called.

The jerboa hesitantly shuffled toward him.

"Listen, jerboa, I have you to thank for helping me scout these newcomers. Did you see that fox?" Boris shook his head in awe. "What agility, what speed! Those coachers are going to flip when they see the squad I've put together!"

Boris's love for the game was so heartfelt that Jerry felt a confusing twinge of enthusiasm. "R-right on, sir," said the jerboa.

On the other end of the marble, spirits weren't so high.

"Oh goodness," said Tobin. "I'm trying my best, I really am. They're just so fast and I can't—"

Dawn stopped the pangolin. "You're not the reason we're behind. We're giving them way too much space to take shots."

The team bowed their heads.

"But we're getting better," she said.

"It's true," agreed Julian. "I'm starting to get the hang of this kiwi. You've got to hold them around the knees."

Ajax shook his head. "But it's not enough. We need something more. A way to keep their defenders from pouncing on the player with the spider. If we can do that, we may just have a chance to score."

"What do you mean?" asked Julian, sensing his friend was onto something.

"I think Ajax is suggesting that it's time for a little coyote hunting magic," said Ciro. "Misdirection and coordination. That's how we'll win this."

Chapter Twenty-Seven
THE RISE OF THE CAPTIVES

"*Andiamo, Andiamo!*" Bismark screamed over the roaring crowd. "Let's go, team!"

The players from both teams took their places on the floor. Boris's team looked relaxed as they stretched and prepared for what they assumed would be an equally dominant second period. The challengers, however, did not look like the same forlorn bunch that had left the floor just minutes earlier.

"Players! To face-off positions! Dingbats, to

center floor," Bismark said with relish.

Dawn and Vee squared up for the face-off.

"Don't worry," jeered the croc, "I'll make it quick."

The fox's whiskers curled, betraying the trace of a smile. The bats dropped the spider.

"Game on!" shouted Bismark.

In a flash, Dawn had Harry in the crook of her kiwi. Then, with a tap, she passed the spider back to Cora.

Just as planned, the wombat glided toward the center line, where she was joined by the rest of her team. In a shoulder-to-shoulder formation, the Nocs barreled forward, a single, straight line of force.

Thwack, Cora tapped the spider back to Ciro. Thwack, Ciro tapped the spider to Dawn. Thwack, Dawn tapped the spider to Ajax. Thwack, Ajax tapped the spider to Julian. By passing just before the defender had a chance to attack, the challengers drove their single line straight down the floor.

Suddenly Boris, standing in goal, was outnumbered five-to-one. Julian raised his kiwi high, winding up to hit Harry with all his might. Boris lunged left, falling for Julian's fake. With a smirk, Julian passed Harry to Dawn who was waiting at the right side of the goal.

With a smooth swipe, she deflected the spider into the corner of the net.

"WZZZZ!" All four bats whistled to mark the stoppage of play, but were drowned out by the roar of the spectators.

"We have ourselves a game, ladies and gentlemen!" Bismark called out. "A point for the challengers! *Un punto* for freedom!"

The Nocs all screamed with delight. Holding their kiwis high, they gathered together for a victorious embrace. They could do this. They could beat the Crocs.

But as the cheering subsided, one fan could still be heard.

"Unbelievable! Brilliant! Magnificent!" Boris screamed in a frenzy. "A sneak attack! A clever display of strategy! I love it!"

"Coach?" Vee asked.

"Oh, excuse me! Got carried away there. Sorry, yes. Too bad, team! Nice try. Let's pull it together. Don't let that one happen again."

The Crocs turned back toward the floor.

"What's going on?" whispered Miss.

"They just scored," murmured Orr, "but Boris seems—"

"—happy," said Vee.

Shaking their heads in confusion, the crocodiles moved back to their posts.

"Face off!" said the bats in chorus as they dropped the spider.

Miss gained control of Harry. She passed him back to Vee, who sheltered the tarantula and kept her passing lanes open. They were not going to get caught off guard by another five-player assault. But this time the challengers moved out of the way. Ciro, Dawn, Cora, Julian, and Ajax all gathered together at the edge of the rink.

Vee and Orr stopped passing. Miss, Hay, and Bee stared in disbelief.

"What are you guys doing over there?" Miss asked the Nocs, approaching them in confusion.

"Yeah, what's the matter?" asked Vee.

"What do you mean?" Cora answered. "Nothing's the matter." The wombat fluttered her lashes.

"But you're all just standing there. You're not trying to stop us," Orr said, pointing out the obvious.

"You know we have possession, right?" asked Vee.

While attention was directed to the sidelines, Tobin crept out from goal. Stealthily, the pangolin made his way down the marble. With a flick of his kiwi, Tobin gained control of Harry, who had been abandoned at center floor. Suddenly, he was facing Boris in a one-on-one showdown.

"Come on, pangolin! Show me the good stuff!" Boris bared his sharp teeth.

All the players whirled around as Tobin raised his kiwi.

Thwack!

Tobin slapped Harry with the rounded side of the kiwi's beak, putting an unusual spin on the spider. Harry curved up, around, and past Boris's shoulder, thunking cleanly into the back of the goal.

"WZZZZ!" The whistles blared out again as the bats raised their wings in the air. The point was good.

"Goooaaal! A second point for the challengers!" Bismark called out above the wild celebration. The jerboas were hopping with excitement. The captured animals clutched each other in disbelief.

"No way! No way" Bee objected "That's...that's cheating?"

The bats gathered together for a moment, then raised their wings again. "Fair goal!" they declared.

"Way to go!" said Julian, patting the pangolin's scales. Tobin blushed.

"You did it!" cried Cora.

175

Dawn glided over to offer her congratulations, but she could not shout over the noise of the audience. The cave was filled with the sound of hundreds of voices screaming as one, their freedom close at hand.

"Unbelievable, ladies and gentlemen!" Bismark exclaimed. "Another *estrategia excelente*! The Nocs have pulled within one, and they look like they want to go all...the...way!"

Yet again, as the crowd noise died down, one euphoric voice was left speaking.

"Spectacular! Unheard of!" Boris wailed. "What a performance! Bravo!"

The Nocs huddled together, staring at their opponent in confusion. Something did not feel right.

"Why is he cheering us on?" asked Ajax.

"Oh goodness, do you think he let in my shot on purpose?" wondered Tobin.

Dawn shook her head. "There's no telling what Boris is thinking. All we can do is keep playing."

The challengers went mute as they considered the possibilities. Boris was still ranting beside the goal.

"Wonderful!" he said. "I will meet those coachers at last! It is only a matter of time!" In his claws he still clenched the strange red tube. Jerry watched from the sidelines as Boris whispered to the object, and then pressed it to his ear, as if it were speaking back.

The second period resumed, but neither team could organize enough to score again. When the whistles blew, the score was Crocs three, Nocs two.

Chapter Twenty-Eight
THE FINAL PERIOD

"Mon dieu, how time flies! Here we are, ladies and gentlemen—the final period has arrived! And here comes the fox who has set this cave on fire tonight! Not literally, of course!" Bismark blew Dawn a kiss as the players emerged from their huddles and fell into position. The floor had been refreshed by lomandra brooms during the intermission.

The jerboa fans were still riled up from Tobin's surprise goal in the second period. Before the bats even whistled to resume play, the crowd was already roaring in anticipation. Boris, too, was stomping his feet and howling like a joyous lunatic.

"*La pièce de la résistance*!" Bismark hollered above the noise. "Game on!"

As the bats dropped the spider, time seemed to slow down. Dawn gripped her kiwi. Tobin bit his tongue. Bismark cleared his throat.

Dawn won the face-off and swept the tarantula over to Cora. Thwack, thwack, thwack! They passed Harry in a triangle, advancing slowly but surely. But Miss was running out of patience. She checked Ajax with her shoulder and stole the spider. The rough play sent a gasp through the crowd. By the time the coyote staggered to his feet, the Crocs were already attacking the goal.

"Oh goodness!" said Tobin. Miss was bearing down on him, her kiwi raised. At the edge of his vision he saw Cora. The wombat tapped her nose. Tobin shut his eyes, and took a deep smell. In the darkness, he could sense a presence. It smelled like kiwi beak and spider, and it was coming his way, curving slightly to the right. He held out his paw.

THOCK!

The crowd went wild, pounding their chests,

ripping hair out of their ears. The sheer excitement made the air ripple. Tobin opened his eyes and looked down. He was holding Harry.

"Oof! Not so tight, pangolin!" shouted the tarantula.

"I'm very sorry," said Tobin, and carefully slid the spider over to Dawn.

Thwack, thwack, thwack! Dawn passed to Cora, who tapped it back to Julian. Julian advanced up the floor, dodging a lunging tackle from Orr.

Thwack, thwack, thwack! Julian flicked a pass up in the air, which soared over Vee's head and landed right at the feet of Ciro.

Thwack, thwack thwack! Ciro tucked the spider between his legs, but he was checked against the side of the rink by Miss. Thwack, thwack, thwack!

"*Mon dieu! Mon dieu!* We have reached the final minute of play!" Bismark shouted. He looked down at his friends. They were still down by one point, and the Crocs controlled the spider. Was it really going to end this way?

The Crocs took a long shot at goal, which Tobin recovered expertly. He passed the tarantula forward to Dawn. The fox looked left, then right. Her teammates were covered by defenders. A pass would be risky.

"Thirty seconds! The time ticks away!" called Bismark.

The bats noted the time and raised their fingers to their mouths, ready to blow the final whistle.

Bismark sat up from his seat. His heart was pounding. "Twenty! *Veinte! Vingt!*"

Dawn glided down the floor, controlling Harry with gentle touches of her kiwi. Two crocodiles peeled away from their marks to defend the charging fox. Just before they converged on her for a crushing tackle, Dawn crouched. The Crocs collided with each other, crumpling to the floor.

"Fifteen seconds! Ladies and gentlemen, do not blink, do not breathe, do not move a muscle! You don't want to miss this!"

Thwack, thwack, thwack! Dawn made a quick pass to Cora, who was wide open. The wombat took it down the marble, where she was met with stiff resistance from Bee. Cora whipped the spider over to Julian, who flicked it back to Ajax. Thwack, thwack, thwack! Ajax passed to Ciro, who passed to Dawn.

Ten seconds. Thwack, thwack, thwack.

The bats inhaled deeply, preparing to whistle for the end of the game.

Thwack, thwack, thwack. Eight seconds.

The challengers raced along the marble floor, frantically trying to outmaneuver their defenders and get open for the pass.

Thwack, thwack, thwack. Seven seconds.

The crowd was quiet. Their fate seemed to be decided.

Thwack, thwack, thwack. Six seconds.

"*Una tragedia*! The end is upon us! And what on earth are those two doing?" Bismark wailed.

Down at the opposite end of the floor, Tobin and Cora stood hand in hand. Then they started to spin, gripping each other's paws, until they were a hypnotic blur of fur and scales. The crowd gasped. Round and round, the spiraling twosome shot down the rink, picking up speed.

Before anyone could react, the spinning sensation of pangolin and wombat whirled in front of Boris's goal. Dawn, who still had control of Harry, had a choice to make.

"Three seconds! Two! One!" shouted Bismark.

Dawn drew her kiwi back, held her breath, and let it rip.

Thwack! Harry careened through the air and bounced off the whirling dervish—whether it was off Tobin or Cora, it was impossible to say—and hit the top-right corner of the goalpost. Tink! The spider landed just outside the goal-line. No goal. Boris gaped at the motionless spider at his feet. Then, before he could blink, there was Dawn who had hustled forward after the pass. Thwick. With a tap of Dawn's kiwi, Harry slid into the net.

The bats were too shocked to whistle. Even if they had, the clamor of the audience would have drowned them out. The shot was good. The game was tied.

Chapter Twenty-Nine
THE SHOOT-OUT

"Oh goodness, now what happens?" asked Tobin. He was still a bit woozy from all the spinning around.

"What a thrilling turn of events!" said Boris. "My heart can't handle it! My cold blood is boiling! A tiebreaker! A shoot-out!"

The Crocs looked at their leader in dismay. Any shred of composure he had at the beginning of the match was long since cast off. He was openly giddy.

"How does this shoot-out work?" asked Dawn.

The bats stepped forward and cleared their throats. Shouting over the crowd had fried their vocal cords.

"Each team will select three players to take a shot on goal."

"If at the end of the shoot-out, a tie still remains, both teams will shoot again."

"Sudden death this time. First goal wins."

"*Svor*."

A concerned expression registered on Dawn's face. She glanced up at Boris, who could barely contain his excitement.

"Boris," she said, "if we win this shootout, we win the game. Correct?"

"Yes, yes, if you win, good for you!" said the ecstatic crocodile.

"Then you will let us all go free?"

Boris turned away from the fox. He swallowed hard and scratched his neck with his kiwi's beak. "Right, right. Everyone, to your positions! Our shooters will be Miss, Vee, and Orr. The Nocs shoot first!"

Dawn did not like the way Boris answered her question, but had no time to argue. The Nocs huddled and quickly selected three canines to be their shooters:

Julian, Ajax, and then Dawn.

The crowd was tense as Julian glided to the center line. He had a nervous habit of spinning his kiwi.

"Oh, Julian, stop, stop I tell you. I'm going to be sick!" the bird begged, her bristly feathers fanning out with each rotation.

"Sorry. I'm just a little nervous."

The coyote squatted down low. The blue light of the cave started to swim and dance before his eyes. A white haze crept in at the edges of his vision.

"WZZZZ!" the bats whistled.

Harry dropped to the marble floor, and Julian tapped the spider forward, picking up speed.

Boris danced side to side, knees up, knees down, moving his body to protect different parts of the net.

Halfway to the goal, Julian flipped Harry straight up into the air. The crowd went silent as they watched the tarantula rise and fall. In one fluid motion, the coyote swung his kiwi like a hammer, connecting with Harry in midair. The spider whizzed toward Boris and bounced off the tip of his outstretched claw. The shot was good.

"WZZZZ!" all four bats blew in unison.

"Goal for the Nocs!" shouted Bismark. "They pull into an early lead. And the pressure, *mes amis,* is most definitely on the Crocs now!"

The crowd howled as Miss slid to the center of the floor. The Croc hunched over her kiwi, shutting out the jeers and boos. When the whistle blew, she cradled Harry with her kiwi and methodically moved down the floor. She switched the tarantula over to her left side. With a slap, the crocodile belted the spider at the corner of the net.

Tobin dove to the left, his stumpy arms fully extended. But as he jumped, his tail caught under his foot.

"Oof!" His legs shot out behind him, sending him into a high-speed front flip. As he came down with a heavy thud on the stone, he felt a hard tap on the side of his rear foot. Blotches and spots danced across his vision. And then everything went black.

"Tobin!" Cora cried.

The Nocs all gathered around their pangolin friend lying unconscious in the goal. Even Bismark glided down from his announcer's perch.

"*Mon ami*! *Mi hermano*!" He flung his arms around his friend. "Oh, Fate, how cruel you are! You bring this wonderful pangolin into my life, only to snatch him away so soon? Yes, he made terrible smells from time to time, but—"

"Bismark," said Dawn, "he's waking up."

"Oh goodness," Tobin moaned, his beady eyes blinking.

"How are you feeling?" Dawn asked. Bending down, she inspected the pangolin's eyes for signs of trauma.

"Oh goodness," Tobin muttered. The swarm of faces around him was shifting into focus. He remembered where he was.

"Move aside, players!" called a bat, swooping in.

"Give him some space," said another, clearing a path through the huddled players.

The pangolin started to stand.

"No need to worry, everybody. I'll be just—ow!" He clutched his right foot. It was swelling to the size of a big, ripe tomato.

"Looks like a sprain," said Dawn. "Do you need to sit this one out?"

Tobin bent his head low, unable to speak aloud the words that they all knew to be true.

"It's all right," whispered Dawn. "You were great, and the game's almost done." The fox cleared her throat and turned to the bats. "I will serve as replacement goalie."

"WZZZZZZ!" the bats whistled. "Then it's

settled! Back to your sidelines, we're on to the next shooter!"

Ciro and Ajax reached toward the pangolin to help him move off the floor.

"Wait!" said Tobin. "Did I miss the block? Did they score?"

Dawn placed a paw on the pangolin's shoulder. Her amber eyes glowed with pride.

"No, Tobin." The fox smiled. "You stopped it. We are winning by one."

Chapter Thirty
THE FINAL SHOT

Ajax and Vee both made their shots, bringing the score to two-one. The Nocs still held the lead. Only one shooter from each team remained.

The bleachers were boiling with anticipation and excitement. The jerboas had screamed themselves hoarse, but they were still going at it. Boris and the rest of the Crocs were bunched together on their end of the floor, trying their best to strategize over the crowd noise.

Over on the Nocs' side of the floor, Dawn

stretched her legs in preparation for her shot. She licked the kiwi's feathers, slicking them down for maximum wind efficiency. She was ready.

On the sidelines, Ciro, Julian, Ajax, Tobin and Cora watched as the fox took center floor. If she made this shot, they would win. They would have their victory and freedom.

Bismark waved his hands, calling for calm. "Ladies and gentlemen! *Silencio, por favor*! The fox is about to work her magic and win this game. Of course, she has already won my heart."

The whistles sounded, and the bats dropped Harry to the marble.

Thwack, thwack. Dawn scooped the spider and thundered down the floor. Thwack, thwack. Boris spread his limbs to cover all four corners of the goal. His tail curled between his legs, protecting against the dummy shot. Thwack, thwack. Dawn was closing in on the goal. She raised the kiwi high above her shoulder, squeezing it a bit tighter than usual.

"Eek!" The bird opened her eyes, spotted Harry, and flinched.

Dawn still managed to connect with the spider, but she shanked the shot wide. Harry banked to the left, arced over Boris, and hit the wall.

"No goal!" said the bats. The crowd became quiet. Whispers filled the room.

"*Mon dieu*! Ladies and gentleman, my fellow nocturnals, what a twist! A malfunction of the equipment at a crucial time! Hearts are breaking here in the cave tonight—but don't lose hope yet, folks. Our Nocs are still one point ahead." Bismark swirled his cape to add drama. The crowd was eating it up. "And it all rides on this last shot!"

Boris's teeth were chattering with nervous excitement. The other Crocs chewed their sharp talons down to dull, stubby points. The reptiles were still in contention.

"Your final shooter!" called the bats.

Orr glided to the center line. If he missed the goal, the Nocs won. If he made it, there would be sudden death.

Standing in the goal, Dawn clenched her jaw. She had to stop this shot, but she knew she lacked the reflexes of a natural goalkeeper. The fox glanced at the sidelines. For some of her teammates, "sudden death" would mean sudden death.

"Oh goodness," Tobin said. He saw Dawn drop her head. She looked like she bore the weight of the world on her shoulders.

193

The bats flapped their wings and flew above center line, ready to blow their whistles.

"Wait!" Tobin shouted out from the sideline. Everyone gasped as the injured pangolin limped out on the floor with his kiwi.

"What are you doing?" asked Dawn. "You've got a sprained foot!"

Tobin looked at the fox. He thought of her strength and her leadership. How she never let anyone down, and was too proud to ask for help. "I can do this," he said. "Let me take care of this one."

Dawn locked eyes with the determined pangolin.

"I know you can," said the fox. She patted Tobin on the scales, and then made her way toward the sideline. "Tobin," she called over her shoulder.

The pangolin met his friend's gaze.

Dawn's whiskers curled up as she smiled. "Thank you," she whispered.

Boris mounted a stone near his bench.

"Enough, already!" he screamed. "On with the game!"

Dawn hurried to the sidelines as Tobin took his position on the goal line.

"WZZZZ!" the bats whistled, and dropped the spider. With gentle flicks of his wrist, Orr controlled the spider by barely touching it with the tip of the kiwi's beak.

Tap.

Tap.

Tap.

Orr moved slowly toward the Noc's goal, letting the pressure build on Tobin.

Tap.

Tap.

Tap.

Seconds felt like hours. Orr seemed to be taunting the pangolin with his slow approach.

Tap.

Tap.

Tap.

The pangolin trembled. "Oh goodness, oh g-goodness," he stammered over and over again. With bad vision and a bad foot, Tobin started to panic.

Tap.

Tap.

Tap.

Tobin glanced at the sideline. He looked at Ciro, Dawn, the coyotes. Their eyes gleamed with hope. Then, he saw Cora. The wombat smiled and touched her nose.

Tap.

Tap.

Tap.

Suddenly, Tobin's foot didn't hurt. The pangolin tightened his grip on his kiwi. "The nose knows. The nose knows." Tobin repeated and braced himself for the shot. "The nose knows!" He closed his eyes.

Tap.

Tap.

Tap.

He was in the dark world again. The crowd felt louder, closer. Tobin took a deep breath. Aromas filtered into his nose, adding color to the darkness. The glowing pools smelled like grass. The jerboas smelled like sweat. And Orr smelled like salt. He could sense the Croc rushing toward him, but he was not scared anymore.

Tap.

Tap.

Tap.

Orr raised his kiwi. The crowd froze in suspense. THWACK!

Harry rocketed through the air, a line drive to the top-right corner of the net. All eyes were glued on the spider. All eyes except for the goalie's.

With his eyes still pressed shut, Tobin waited. He could smell a small object approaching. Sniff, sniff.

There was an odd vinegar smell to spiders. He used to find it quite unpleasant, but somehow he had gained a new appreciation. Sniff, sniff.

Strangely, the tarantula seemed to smell slightly sweeter when it was spinning to the left, rather than to the right. Tobin had no idea why this might be. But he could detect a hint of that sweetness now. Sniff, sniff.

He extended his left paw.

THOCK!

Orr stood motionless. The challengers held their breath. And the jerboas went wild.

"WZZZZZZZ!" four whistles blasted, marking the end of the game.

"No goal!" said the bats. "No goal!"

Deafening cheers filled the room and echoed down the stone halls. The Sea Sparkle shone extra bright. The cave lit up with joy.

All of the Nocs swarmed the floor and hoisted Tobin on their shoulders.

"We did it!" they shouted. "We won!"

The jerboas and the other kidnapped animals rushed to congratulate the winning team. Joe ran up to his sister and gave her a long, tearful hug. Audrey nuzzled Ajax with her nose. The mink, possum, raccoon, and honey badger thanked their saviors.

Only the Crocs team remained off to the side, sulking and furious. Except for Boris, of course. Long after the rest of the animals calmed down, he was still clapping and shouting. Dawn approached the jubilant crocodile with her tail held high.

"Good game," she said with a smile. Then she turned to the rest of the Crocs. "Well done." The fox bowed as a sign of respect.

Boris grinned.

"And thank you," continued the fox.

"For what?" Boris asked.

"For agreeing to the terms of the game. For granting us freedom to leave."

The crocodile's snout twitched, and his eyes flickered. "What?" he roared. "You're not going anywhere! I need you!"

"Of course we're going," said Dawn. "That was our deal."

"Never trust a crocodile," said Boris. He flipped the strange red tube up in the air.

For once, Dawn found herself speechless. Boris was breaking his word. Her mouth hung ajar.

"I must meet the coachers!" Boris shouted. "The coachers! Don't you understand? Finally, I am a coacher with a great team!"

The fox's eyes were wide with confusion. "Yes..." she began. "You're a coach, but...."

"No!" screamed the Croc. "A coacher! A coacher!" Boris wrung his claws in the air. "Enough of this! Miss, Bee, Hay, Vee, Orr! Seize them all! Block the exits! They're not going anywhere."

Chapter Thirty-One
SHELL-SHOCKED

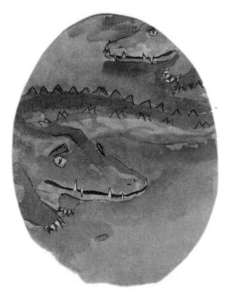

"We are doomed! Done for! Goners!" The sugar glider thrashed around on the floor of the chamber, wailing at the top of his lungs.

"Bismark, stand up," said the fox. "There's not enough space for this right now."

The room was crowded indeed. After Boris's outburst, the Crocs sealed the exits and seized all the animals. Every nocturnal, from the kiwis to the coyotes, had been marshaled into one of the cave's smallest chambers. There was little room to stand, and the heat was becoming unbearable.

"How long will he keep us here?" asked Cora. She put a comforting paw on her brother's quivering shoulder.

Dawn shook her head. There was no way to know.

"I don't understand," said Tobin. "Why was Boris calling himself a coacher?"

"*Oui*! I am tired of not understanding what he means half the time," said Bismark. The sugar glider was still lying on the ground. "He's gone *loco*, I tell you. The croc has gone *loco*!"

"What was that?" roared a voice.

The boulder blocking the entrance rolled aside.

Boom. Boom.

In stomped Boris, his eyes gleaming with fury. Behind him were the five other crocs. Shoulder to shoulder, they stood blocking the passageway.

Dawn stepped forward.

"Don't you move!" yelled the croc.

The fox paused. Something was different about Boris. She took another step forward.

"Stop that!" Boris screamed. "Don't you come any closer! I can't let you leave, don't you understand?"

"We had a deal," said Dawn.

"Yes. A deal," he repeated. The crocodile paused and turned his head. He opened his claws and stared down at the red tube, as if it held all the answers. He tossed it up in the air.

This was it. A brief moment of opportunity. A chance to regain control.

Instinctively, the fox pounced.

"Grrrr!" Dawn snarled. She leapt across Boris's chest, and then, with a swipe of her paw, she snatched the red tube in midair.

"Hey!" Boris cried. "Give that back!"

Dawn raced toward the rear of the room and mounted a stone. "Give our freedom back and I will!" The fox looked at the object. "Tell me, Boris—what is this?"

"Stop! Be careful! Don't break it!" Boris was whimpering now. "It's—it's all they left me!"

Dawn turned the tube over in her paws, inspecting it closely. It had a certain unnatural quality, as if it did not belong in their world.

"Please," begged the crocodile. Boris fell to his knees. "It's from the coachers."

Dawn climbed down from her stone and approached the crocodile. "Boris, these 'coachers'... what did they do?" she asked.

Boris's breathing was heavy, and his shoulders

were shaking. Tears dripped onto the hard white marble. "It was last winter," he said. "I woke up from a nap, and everyone was gone. Everyone. My mother, my father, my brothers, my sisters. The coachers took them, because they saw them playing the game out on the swamp ice."

Dawn nodded. She looked again at the tube.

"We've practiced all year," Boris said. "But they never came back. They never came for more players…." The crocodile choked back a sob.

The room buzzed with whispers. The animals were conflicted. Boris had taken them prisoner, after all. But now, as he cried, it was difficult not to feel a little sorry for him.

Boris looked at the hundreds of captives. "That's why I took you all," he said. "I had to find my own players and form my own team. I had to become a coacher!"

Dawn stood before Boris. Despite the sympathy welling up inside her, she knew she had to remain firm. "We cannot help you, Boris."

"But you can!" he insisted. "I just need a good team! When I've got that, those coachers will come to take them, and I can trade my squad and get my family back! Don't you see how simple it is?"

Dawn bowed her head. "It was not 'coachers'

204

who took your family, Boris." Suddenly, everything made sense to the fox. She remembered a word she had heard spoken in whispers when she was just a pup. A word that went hand in hand with another: death. The red cylinder in her paw had taken on a different meaning.

"What are you talking about?" asked Boris. "The coachers left that behind. The other crocodile families kept saying that it was a 'sure sign of coachers,' that the coachers must have come and taken my family." He paused. "That's how I figured it out. That's how I know it's all about the game. The coachers took them because they were such good players."

"Boris," said Dawn. She rolled the red-and-gold tube to his feet. "Your family was taken by 'poachers,' not 'coachers.' I'm not sure why you confused those two words. You must have misheard. But I know this. Your family is gone."

Boris opened his mouth to protest, but Dawn spoke first. "I'm sorry," she said. "I'm sorry for what you have been through. But now you've taken us from our families, our homes, our lives. How are you any better than those poachers who have harmed you?"

Boris stared at the red cylinder on the floor. He looked up and saw the faces of all those he had wronged: the kiwis and the coyotes, the wombats and the jerboas.

Harry. It had all been for nothing. "But... but...." His entire body trembled in protest, but he could no longer deny what was true.

The crocodile snatched up his false treasure. His flawed symbol of family and hope. Then, slowly, he closed his claws. He locked his teeth together and clenched his fist. The shell dropped to the ground with a sound that seemed too small, too light, for what had happened.

Chapter Thirty-Two
A CHANGE OF HEART

Boris sniffled and wiped his long, tear-streaked snout. Then, without saying a word, the crocodile slumped toward the door, his tail dragging behind him.

"Boris," said Dawn.

The reptile glanced over his scaly shoulder.

"You don't have to do this anymore." She paused. "You don't have to be alone."

The crocodile hung his head. "I have no choice," he insisted. "My family—"

"No," said the fox. "A terrible thing happened to you, that is true. But we all must face hardship and pain. Look at these animals." She gestured to the silent crowd around her. "Everyone here has been challenged. But they have dealt with this challenge together." She took a step forward. "They are together. We are together. You are only separate from us because you've chosen to be."

Boris looked at the room full of animals. They were tall and short, thick and thin. He saw bristly feathers, silken fur, and tough scales. Some hailed from the plains, others from the forests, some from the valleys. They were different, all of them. But they stood together.

"It couldn't be true." Boris sobbed and sobbed. "Maybe a part of me knew the truth all along, but I just couldn't let it be true! I had to believe it was about the game." The crocodile sank to the floor, overcome with exhaustion and shame. "I'm sorry," he whispered. "I'm so sorry."

Dawn rested her paw on Boris's shoulder. "We must all face our truths," she declared. "If we don't, we can never move on."

There was a long, thoughtful silence as the animals considered these words.

"I have a truth." A soft voice filled the air.

Everyone turned. It was Cora.

"This might be silly, but, well…." The wombat gulped. "I kind of liked playing that game."

The fox raised her brows. Boris sniffled and wiped his eyes.

"Now that you mention it," said the mink, "so did I."

"I did, too!" added Audrey, the coyote. "Though I hated the way we were brought here."

There were shouts of wholehearted agreement.

The honey badger raised his paw. So did Ajax and Julian. One by one, a wave of others did, too. Then Harry crept forward.

"With all due respect," said the tarantula, rubbing his bruised exoskeleton, "I absolutely despised it!"

The animals could not help but laugh.

"We did, too!" Twelve worn kiwis agreed with Harry.

"How about you, Tobin?" The fox looked at the pangolin. He was rubbing his claws together. "Did you like it?"

"Oh g-goodness," he stammered. "I…I liked parts of it."

Dawn nodded. "As did I," she admitted.

"Have you forgotten about *moi*?" asked

209

Bismark, clutching his chest as if gravely wounded. "I was kidnapped, too, you know! Does my opinion not matter because I was not down on the floor? I tell you, being the announcer is hard work. The game cannot be played without the *maestro* calling out every goal!" He flourished his cape. "Though I suppose I did quite enjoy it."

"Well, I, for one, would keep playing," said Audrey.

"Yes," the honey badger agreed. "So would I. And I bet my sister would love it too, if I could leave this place to go get her."

"I'd keep playing," said Julian.

"Me too," grunted Ajax.

"So would I," said the mink.

"I'm in!" said the possum.

An excited buzz filled the room.

Boris stood back on his feet. "You mean, you'd stay?" asked the crocodile. "You mean, you might... forgive me?" The crocodile looked hopefully at the crowd of nocturnals.

"Not so fast," said Ajax.

"That's right," agreed Julian. "You don't go from captor to comrade so quickly!"

"But," said the fox, "there is no reason you cannot stay."

"We'll just have to appoint a new coach," said the mink.

"And a nurse!" said the possum.

"I could do that," offered Audrey. "And I could mend the broken equipment as well."

"No way!" balked the kiwis. "We're not your 'equipment' any more. We're leaving!" The birds riffled their feathers in protest.

"Me too!" said the spider. He cradled his sore seventh leg. "I'm outta here!"

"Well, maybe you could use sticks instead?" Dawn suggested. "And rocks instead of Harry."

"Thought of that," said a kiwi. He rubbed his beak. "Believe me… thought of that."

"But alas," said another. "Sticks break too easily on the marble. You'd need a near-endless supply."

"Same with the rocks," Harry said. "They'll split open every other game."

Everyone mumbled and sighed, disheartened by this apparent dead end. Everyone, that is, except Dawn.

"Boris," she said. "Would you like to stay here with everyone?"

The crocodile nodded vigorously.

"You're strong and you know these caves well."

Again, Boris nodded.

"Why don't you become head of equipment? It'd be your job to gather rocks and sticks for the games," she suggested.

"We'd need a continuous supply," said Ajax.

"That's right," said the fox. "It would show real solidarity. Real valor."

Boris exhaled through his nostrils and considered all he had done. He looked at the crowd of nocturnals whom he'd napped, held captive, and threatened. He thought about their proposition. Serving as head of equipment would be hard, grueling work. Endless treks up and down from the surface. Heavy, unwieldy loads of sticks. But, strangely enough, this thought made him feel less tired. Less burdened. Less lonely.

"I'll do it!" he cried. "Please, let me do it!"

"Will you work honorably?" asked the fox.

"I will," promised Boris. He placed a claw over his heart in respect.

Dawn nodded, confirming the crocodile's new post.

Ajax flashed a cheeky grin. "Well, what're you waiting for? Get us some sticks!"

Chapter Thirty-Three
ARRIVEDERCI, AMIGOS!

"Players and spectators! Athletes and *amigos*! It is with great sadness, and significant inner conflict, that I resign my post as announcer. As much as I would like to entertain the masses, the Brigade must go. There are others who need our help! I bid you *adieu*." Bismark took a deep bow. "*Au revoir! Adios! Arrivederci!*"

Jerry hopped to his side. "Maybe I could take over?"

"*Excusez-moi?*" said the sugar glider. "Don't

be ridiculous! Oh, my silly, miniscule mate, you could not be the *maestro*! Only I possess that rare talent." With a flick of his paw, Bismark dismissed the jerboa. "*Solamente yo!*"

"Oh, well, I just thought..."

"You thought wrong, *mon ami!*"

"Jerry," said Dawn. She approached the rejected jerboa. "I have a favor to ask of you."

"Yes, yes! Of course!" Jerry glanced at the sugar glider. "I can be useful."

Dawn pointed at a mound of lomandra leaves. "I'd like you to use these to form a trail through the caves," she explained. "That way, the path out will be clearly marked. All animals, players, and spectators should be able to come and go as they please."

"Yes, ma'am!" replied Jerry. The jerboa started at once, motioning for a few friends to assist him.

Bismark breathed a sigh of relief. Finally, a moment alone with Dawn!

"You know, *mon amour*, my lovely Dawn, I have been meaning to speak with—"

"Look out below!" called the bats. They dove down from the ceiling, splashing Bismark with a faceful of blue water as they landed in the glowing pool.

"Ahhhh, that feels nice!" sighed a bat.

The foursome scrubbed off their referee colors.

"Looks better, too," said another.

"Stripes are so last season," said a third.

"*Svor*."

Tobin giggled at the yammering bats. They were having fun—how long had it been since he had seen anyone having carefree fun?

"I still can't believe how beautiful this place is."

The pangolin turned to see Cora. She was standing beside him, gazing at the glimmering pools. He smiled. "Yes," he said. "It really is."

The wombat bowed her head, attempting to conceal her flushed cheeks. "Are you…leaving?" she asked.

Tobin nodded. "Are you…staying?"

Cora nodded as well. "Joe is here," she explained. "I need to be with my family."

"And I, with my Brigade," said the pangolin.

For a moment, the duo stood silent, absorbing their pending departure. Tobin reached under his scales and pulled out a piece of snakeskin that had fallen loose from his cape.

"So you remember," he said. Carefully, the pangolin tied a comfortable knot around Cora's wrist.

The wombat smiled at her new snakeskin

bracelet. She gazed up at Tobin. "I could never forget."
Cora stood on her toes. Then she leaned toward Tobin,
turned up her nose, and planted a little kiss on his cheek.

Wearing a smile the length of his tail, Tobin
watched Cora run toward her brother. "Oh goodness,"
he sighed.

"Pangolin!" shouted the sugar glider. "Don't
you agree it's impossible?"

"Hmm?" asked Tobin, snapping out of his
daydream. "What's impossible?"

"To replace me as the announcer!" Bismark
sighed with exasperation. "Jerry thinks he can do it,
but that's *absolument* absurd. Just a meaningless rodent
fantasy. Jerry as *maestro*," he scoffed. "They would be
better off with nobody doing the job!"

As if he had been summoned, the jerboa scurried
up to the group. "All set for you, ma'am!" he announced.
"The path is being marked as we speak."

"Good work," replied Dawn.

The little animal grinned.

"And Jerry," Dawn added, "thank you. Thank
you for staying with us."

"Might stick around some more!" the jerboa
mumbled. "I hear there's a job up for grabs."

The sugar glider rolled his big, round eyes.

"Yes," he snapped. "Always need spectators."

Jerry twitched his nose, and then hopped away toward the stands.

Boom. Boom.

Boris came thumping down the hall.

He dumped a bundle of long sticks onto a growing pile.

Miss, Bee, Hay, Vee, and Orr marched behind him, each carrying an armful of rounded stones. The work seemed to be doing them good. The crocodiles were smiling and laughing.

"Well, *ça va*, my *amigos*!" said Bismark. "We came, we saw, and we conquered."

Tobin looked at the roomful of animals, happy, joyful, and free. "We did it," he said.

Dawn glanced to her left at the pangolin, and then to her right at the sugar glider. There they stood. The members of the Nocturnal Brigade. The bold and fearless three. "Yes," said the fox with a smile, "we did."

"Shall we then?" said the sugar glider. He pointed to the path leading out. "Onward and upward!"

Without waiting for a reply, Bismark began his ascent toward the surface. Tobin crept slowly behind him, shuffling along the lomandra leaves. But the fox lingered behind.

The pangolin glanced over his shoulder. "Aren't you coming?" he asked.

Reluctantly, Dawn nodded. But just as she lifted her paw to leave, the fox felt a presence behind her. She turned. There he was, the regal coyote.

"Dawn…" started Ciro.

"Ciro," Dawn finished.

Neither animal knew what to say next. Instead, the canines stood in silence, their heads close and eyes locked.

"Ahem!" Bismark interrupted the scene from above. "Dawn? My lady? My sweet? What's going on down there? The carnivore's not coming with us, is he?"

"Not this time," she said. With her eyes still on Ciro, the fox slowly stepped back. "It's just us Brigade-mates for now."

Ciro smiled and watched as the fox caught up with her friends. "For now," he repeated. Then, with a whoosh of his wiry, gray tail, he trotted toward his fellow coyotes.

Back in their threesome, the Nocturnal Brigade reached the outcropping where they'd first laid their eyes on the shiny floor.

"It looks different, doesn't it?" said the pangolin.

Dawn peered over the edge to see animals bustling across the marble. Already, the wombats and the coyotes were running new drills on the floor, while the jerboas cheered from the stands. Meanwhile, near a pool, Miss, Bee, Hay Vee, and Orr were rehearsing the rules of the game for their jobs as referees. Boris was running full-speed, gathering more supplies.

With everyone free and together, the cavern felt vibrant and warm. Even the glow of the Sea Sparkle seemed to shine a bit brighter.

Dawn gazed at the scene one last time. Then she turned to her two, loyal friends. "We are not alone," she said. "Any of us."

With heads held high, the Brigade made their way toward the surface. As they squeezed into the tight tunnel that led to the riverside, a faint voice echoed up from below.

"Ladies and gentlemen! Welcome to the game!"

Bismark punched the dirt. "That scoundrel!" he yelled. "That imposter! Up to his old tricks again, I see!"

Tobin padded up to the sugar glider. "Don't worry," he said reassuringly. "He doesn't have your special talents!"

The sugar glider took a deep breath. "You're

right, of course, *mi amigo*. The jerboa lacks my unique flair! A true announcer needs wit! Worldliness! An extensive and complex vocabulary."

The pangolin and the fox nodded. Then the voice rang out once again.

"I am Jerry," said the jerboa, "your multilingual *m-maestro*! *Hola*! *Bonjour*! *Sh-sh-shalom*!"

Bismark's jaw dropped in horror. "My goodness! My gracious! *Mon dieu*!"

THE NOCTURNALS

Bonus Content

*

Character Animal Glossary

*

Discussion Questions for Your Book Club

*

Q&A with Author Tracey Hecht

*

Character Animal Glossary

Coyote
Scientific Name: *Canis latrans*
Common Name: Coyote
Physical Characteristics: gray upper parts with white throat and belly; reddish brown forelegs, sides of head, muzzle and feet; long, black-tipped guard hairs on shoulder area; drooping tail with black tip; pointed, erect ears; eyes with yellow iris and round pupil; black nose; excellent senses of hearing and smell
Behavioral Characteristics: nocturnal; form packs; dig or find burrows for dens; can run up to 65 km/hour and jump as far as 4 m; very vocal; secretive
Diet: rabbits, squirrels, and mice, birds, snakes, insects, fruits, vegetables; prefer fresh meat but will consume carrion and human trash
Map: species found throughout North and Central America
Habitat: extremely adaptable to forests, grasslands, deserts, and swamps
Major Threats: No current threats
Status: Least Concern

Crocodile
Scientific Name: *Crocodylus porosus*
Common Name: Saltwater crocodile
Physical Characteristics: Males up to 7 m long; females up to 3 m long; large head with a pair of ridges running from eyes along center of snout; oval-shaped scales; young have pale yellow backs with black stripes and spots; adults have darker backs with lighter tan or gray areas; underside is white or yellow; tail is gray with dark bands; heavyset jaw with 64-68 teeth
Behavioral Characteristics: hide in water when hunting with only eyes and nostrils exposed; lunge to capture prey; eat under water; strong swimmer that can swim very far from land; bark to communicate
Diet: young prey on insects and small amphibians, crustaceans, fish and reptiles; adults eat larger prey, including buffalo, wild boar, and monkeys

Map: species most commonly found on coasts of northern Australia and islands of New Guinea and Indonesia
Habitat: coastal waters or around rivers; freshwater rivers, billabongs, and swamps
Major Threats: Habitat loss from coastal development; hunting and poaching
Status: Least Concern, though Threatened in some areas

Jerboa
Scientific Name: *Euchoreutes naso*
Common Name: Long-eared jerboa
Physical Characteristics: body length of 7-9 cm with tail that is 15-16 cm long; reddish yellow upper body; white belly; tail covered with short hairs and has white or black tuft on the end; hind foot is 4-4.6 cm long and has five digits; ears are one-third longer than head
Behavioral Characteristics: nocturnal; dig burrows; hunt at night; bathe in dust as a form of chemical communication; may use sounds or vibrations to communicate
Diet: flying insects
Map: species found in southernmost Mongolia and regions of north-western China
Habitat: sandy valleys covered with low-growing bushes; cold, high-elevation desert or semi-arid desert regions
Major Threats: no major threats
Status: Least Concern

Pangolin
Scientific Name: *Manis javanica*
Common Name: Malayan pangolin
Physical Characteristics: covered from just above nostrils to tips of tails by many rows of hard, overlapping, movable, sharp-tipped scales; 79-88 cm long, including the prehensile tail; scales on back and sides are olive-brown to yellow; underbelly and face are white; skin is bluish gray; small, conical heads
Behavioral Characteristics: nocturnal; mainly solitary; timid; climbs trees; moves fast when threatened; strong digger
Diet: ants and termites

Map: species found in southeastern Asia within the Indomalayan regions
Habitat: primary and secondary forests, open savannah country, areas vegetated with thick bush, gardens and plantations
Major Threats: hunting and poaching
Status: Critically Endangered

Red Fox
Scientific Name: *Vulpes vulpes*
Common Name: Red fox
Physical Characteristics: pale yellowish red to deep reddish brown coat on top with white or ashy underside; lower parts of legs usually black, tail has white or black tip, dark brown or black nose; body length is 45.5-90 cm and tail length is 30-55 cm
Behavioral Characteristics: nocturnal; solitary; often live in dens abandoned by other animals; can run up to 48 km/h and jump up to 2 m high; stay in same home range entire life
Diet: rodents, rabbits, insects, fruit, carrion
Map: species located throughout much of the Northern Hemisphere from the Arctic Circle to Central America, the steppes of central Asia, and northern Africa
Habitat: forest, tundra, prairie, desert, mountains, farmlands, and urban areas
Major Threats: loss of habitat
Status: Least Concern

Sugar Glider
Scientific Name: *Petaurus breviceps*
Common Name: Sugar glider
Physical Characteristics: head and body 12-13 mm; tail 15-48 mm; bluish-gray back with pale front; dark stripe down back to end of nose; stripes on side of face; gliding membrane from outer side of fore foot to ankle of rear foot; scent glands on forehead and chest
Behavioral Characteristics: nocturnal; spread limbs to open gliding membrane to glide up to 45 meters; nest in groups; territorial; males mark members of group with scent glands; use sounds to communicate with each other

Diet: pollen, nectar, insects and larvae, arachnids, small vertebrates
Map: species found in New Guinea and certain nearby islands, Bismark Archipelago, and northern and eastern Australia
Habitat: forests of all types
Major Threats: no major threats
Status: Least Concern

Wombat
Scientific Name: *Lasiorhinus krefftii*
Common Name: Northern hairy-nosed wombat
Physical Characteristics: thick, stock body about 1 m long; large head with small eyes and pointed ears; covered with soft, silky brown coat; long whiskers; continuously growing upper molars; bad eyesight but good senses of hearing and smell
Behavioral Characteristics: nocturnal; solitary; construct tunnel systems in deep sand; like to sunbathe close to tunnels
Diet: grass
Map: species found in Epping Forest National Park in Central Queensland, Australia
Habitat: live above and below ground in semi-arid, open woodlands or grasslands
Major Threats: loss of habitat and competition with livestock for food
Status: Critically Endangered

The information in the glossary was created through research on the IUCN Red List of Threatened Species (http://www.iucnredlist.org/) and the University of Michigan's Museum of Zoology Animal Diversity Web (http://animaldiversity.org/).

Discussion Questions for Your Book Club

1. Dawn, Bismark and Tobin make up a team, the Nocturnal Brigade. How did the Brigade meet? What qualities do each of those three characters possess that help make them work so well together? Do they have qualities that might hurt the team?

2. The book takes place at night and all of the characters are nocturnal. Can you think of reasons it might be good for animals to be awake at night? Can you think of characteristics in Dawn, the fox, Bismark, the sugar glider and Tobin, the pangolin that are important to their nighttime survival?

3. If you were to pick one character from *The Mysterious Abductions* who is the most like you, who would it be and why? Who is the most unlike you and why? Which character from the book would you most want as your friend and why?

4. What are your favorite locations in the book and why? If you could visit the world of The Nocturnal Brigade, which things from the book would you most want to see? Where do you think these animals might live in the real world?

5. Bismark is an outspoken character. He boasts about his own superior qualities and his affections for Dawn. Do you think Bismark is actually a confident character? If so, why? If no, why not?

6. Dawn is the leader of the Brigade. What does she do to bring the animals together as a team? What does she do when she meets Ciro, the coyote? How does she talk to Boris, the crocodile when she meets him? Do the animals respect her?

7. When Tobin first meets Cora, the wombat, Cora is afraid to speak. How does Tobin try to coax her out of her shyness? What things could you reveal about yourself that might make someone in your life feel less shy around you?

8. Why don't Dawn and Bismark trust Jerry, the jerboa? What does he do to the Brigade that makes them worry about his character? Does he redeem himself in the book?

9. Bismark speaks many languages, as do the bats. What languages are in the book? Are you able to give examples of phrases in any of these languages? Can you come up with some new phrases that Bismark might say? Can you come up with some that the bats might say?

10. Explain the rules of NOC HOC. Which animals are used as equipment in the game? Discuss the actions of the offense and defense.

11. What happens to Boris in the final scenes of *The Mysterious Abductions*? What are the other characters' responses to his actions? How would you have handled Boris?

12. What things in the book would you have done like the Brigade? What things would you have done differently?

13. Discuss the meaning of poaching and endangered species in the wild. Are any of the animals endangered species? Why is poaching wrong? How do both affect the environment?

Q&A with Tracey Hecht

What surprised you the most while writing The Nocturnals?
How much I like the research! Learning about unusual animals is one of the most fun things about the series. I love using the physical traits and unique characteristics of the animals to help develop characters and enhance plot. The details I learn about the nocturnal world are constantly engaging and inspiring me.

Why did you choose the pangolin, fox, and sugar glider for your three main characters? Who is your favorite?
I chose a fox because they're such interesting and cool animals. A pangolin because they are so unusual and physically captivating. And the sugar glider because…well, that's a secret! I constantly change my mind in regards to my favorite character, but outside of the brigade, I do love Cora in this book.

Why did you choose the critically endangered pangolin as a main character?
Spend 10 minutes watching YouTube videos or reading about pangolins and you'll understand why I had to have one as a member of the brigade. Everything about the pangolin is fascinating, their physical traits, their behaviors, their appearance. Plus, despite being the most illegally traded animal in the world, very few people know about the pangolin. Hopefully Tobin will help raise awareness for his amazing species.

Why did you base the book on Australia?
It's based on Australia? I thought it was a fictitious place! Most nocturnal animals are from hot, dry places- Africa, Australia, South East Asia, India. We draw from all of them.

THE NOCTURNALS

Why did you become a writer?
I've always been a writer, since I was young. I was an English/Creative Writing major in college and found jobs even from early on in entertainment and marketing that allowed me to write. I love to create stories, and even more I love to create characters.

How and when do you write?
I need to carve time and space out of my schedule to write. Quiet, open time and space, and for a sustained period. My ideal writing dynamic is from about 5:30 am until about 10 am at the kitchen table of my house in Maine. Everyone in my family sleeps late so I get to be all alone. As I write, I watch and listen to the day wake up all around me. It's perfection. I do that everyday except for Sundays when I let myself sleep in. I love Sundays too!

What is your favorite hobby when you're not writing?
It depends on the season. I like a curled-up-in-front-of-the-fire winter day, a great book, a movie, doing something cozy. I love the summer when I'm in my home in Maine, spending my time outdoors hiking and swimming and cooking over a fire late into the night. One of my favorite things to do is to paddle board on a glassy lake under a sky full of stars. I also adore New York City in the fall—shopping, walking the streets and eating out. My hobbies really do change based on the season.

Acknowledgements

Most things start with the help and kindness of a friend, and with this book the friend was Dean Kehler. I then met Jane Stine, who I would happily dine with at Periyali any day of the week. After Jane came Susan Lurie, our amazing Susan Lurie! Susan who makes the work stronger and the process great fun. Kevin O'Connor came along soon after that, and thank goodness both for his introduction to Julie Schaper and the wonderful team at Consortium as well as to Stacey Ashton. Stacey makes more happen in an hour than I do in a week and I hope never to be without her. Then to Kate Liebman who was interwoven throughout this, doing an unprecedented number of illustrations that I think are among the most beautiful images for any book I've ever seen. To Bailey Carr for our favorite hours each week. To Debra Drodvillo, Jill Vinitsky, Suzy Jurist and Jacques LeMaitre who make the package pretty. To Lauren Wohl, Deb Shapiro, Kate Lied, Wiley Saichek and Mary McAveney who teach me all the most important things and then help me do them. To Lisette Farah, Nina Passero and Joe Gervasi who keep it all running.

And then to our writers' room. A thanks like no other. To Tommy Fagin, Sarah Fieber, Rumur Dowling, Danai Kadzere and Carl Cota-Robles. I like to create, but I love to collaborate, and you make this work what it is. I hope over time I can give back to each of you even half of what I have received. Your series' are next.

Then of course, as with all stories, there are the ones who do the really heavy lifting, the family and friends. Leo, Claire, Nina, Katie, Blair, Stella, Emma, Kelley, Olivia, Mack, JT, Lee, Mom and Dad. Lisa, Michael, Barbara, Michael, Marc. Jess, Lex, Erin and Philip. Thank you for being where I go when it's good and also when it's bad.

And then lastly, though of course he is also the beginning and the middle and everything in between, my thanks to David.

Thank you, so much, to all of you.

About the Author

Tracey Hecht is a writer and entrepreneur who has written, directed and produced several films and founded multiple businesses. Her company Fabled Films is releasing The Nocturnals.

About the Illustrator

Kate Liebman is an artist who lives and works in New York City. She graduated from Yale University, contributes to the Brooklyn Rail, and has shown her work at various galleries.

About Fabled Films

Fabled Films is a publishing and entertainment company creating original content for middle grade and YA audiences. Fabled Films Press combines strong literary properties with high quality production values to connect books with generations of parents and their children. Each property is supported with additional content in the form of animated web series and social media as well as websites featuring activities for children, parents, bookstores, educators and librarians.

FABLED FILMS PRESS
New York City

www.fabledfilms.com

The Adventures Continue in Book 2 of
The Nocturnals

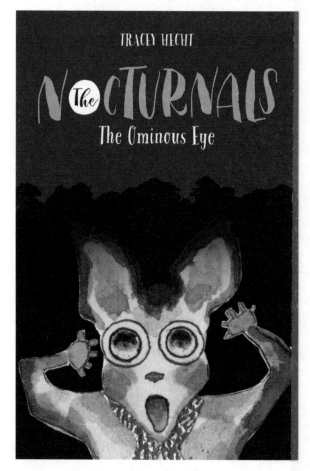

Visit nocturnalsworld.com to watch animated videos, and
download fun nighttime activities!

*

Teachers and Librarians get Common Core Language Arts and
Next Generation Science guides for the book series.

*

#NocturnalsWorld